One That Got Away

Hades' Spawn Motorcycle Club, Volume 2

Lexy Timms

Published by Dark Shadow Publishing, 2015.

ONE THAT GOT AWAY

Hades' Spawn Motorcycle Club Series
Book 2
By
Lexy Timms
Copyright 2015 by Lexy Timms

Hades' Spawn Motorcycle Club Series

One You Can't Forget
Book 1
One That Got Away
Book 2
One That Came Back
Book 3
Coming Fall 2015

Find Lexy Timms:

Lexy Timms Newsletter:
http://eepurl.com/9i0vD
Lexy Timms Facebook Page:
https://www.facebook.com/SavingForever
Lexy Timms Website:
http://lexytimms.wix.com/savingforever
Cover by Book Cover By Design

Description

From Best Selling Author, Lexy Timms, comes a motorcycle club romance that'll make you want to buy a Harley and fall in love all over again.

Emily Rose Dougherty had only fallen in love once, in high school with a boy her parents didn't approve of. Emily saw through the tough-guy façade, his leather jacket, and motorcycle. She gave her heart to him. An accident on Luke's motorcycle brought things to a screeching halt when her parents forbade her to see him again.

Neither forgot about the other.

Fast forward ten years...

Luke Wade built a good life as the owner of a motorcycle repair shop and the road captain of Hades' Spawn Motor Cycle Club. When he reconnects with his high school love, Emily, things seem to be falling into place.

When dirty dealings within Hades' Spawn, problems created by Emily's ex-boyfriend and secrets from Luke's past threaten to blow Luke's life and his relationship with Emily apart, it suddenly feels like everything spiraling out of control.

Can Luke and Emily find a way to conquer the obstacles to their love or will they be to each other, "the one that got away?"

This is book 2 of the Hades' Spawn Motorcycle Club Series.

*This story will end on a cliffhanger

* Intended for mature audiences only *

Also by Lexy Timms

Hades' Spawn Motorcycle Club
One You Can't Forget
One That Got Away

Heart of the Battle Series
Celtic Viking
Celtic Rune
Celtic Mann

Managing the Bosses Series
The Boss

Saving Forever
Saving Forever - Part 1
Saving Forever - Part 2
Saving Forever - Part 3
Saving Forever - Part 4
Saving Forever - Part 5
Saving Forever - Part 6

Southern Romance Series
Little Love Affair
Siege of the Heart
Freedom Forever
Soldier's Fortune

Tennessee Romance
Whisky Lullaby

The University of Gatica Series

The Recruiting Trip
Faster
Higher
Stronger

Standalone
Wash
Loving Charity
Summer Lovin'
Love & College
Billionaire Heart
First Love

Chapter One

The Red Bull

Gibs made his one phone call to Luke, which Luke thought ruefully was both stupid and smart at the same time. It could never be good to let your employer know you were in trouble with the law. On the other hand, Gibs was smart enough to know he could count on Luke.

Luke shook his head. Gibs should have called his wife instead of his boss. It made Luke wonder why he would call him. Was Gibs involved with something he didn't want his wife to know about?

It didn't matter. Luke got no answers at the Westfield Police Department. The only information he did learn was that Gibs had to appear in front of a judge before he could post bond to get out of jail. A chill ran through Luke when he heard that. In Connecticut, misdemeanors could bond out at the police station, but felonies had bond set at the arraignment. Luke scratched his head. In all the years he'd known Gibs, the man didn't do one thing to cross a line. Now he was charged with a felony? It didn't make sense.

All this shit with the club wasn't making any sense to Luke. First Okie was sent to prison, now Gibs had found himself in trouble? When Luke first joined Hades' Spawn, all the riders were straight shooting citizens. Well, maybe not clean and perfect, but close enough in his opinion. However, something was sideways now. In the five years previous he'd been with the club no one strayed on the wrong side of the law. Except for Okie.

It had grown dark when he finally climbed onto his bike and headed home. The spring evening had cooled, and he shivered as the chilly air whipped through him. He decided he would go to the courthouse in the morning and find out what he could. He needed to know what was going on.

His phone vibrated in his pocket, but he couldn't answer it driving, so he waited until he got home to check who called. Luke quirked an eyebrow as he stared at the contact number. *Aces?* Why would he call Luke? "Hey," said Luke. "Calling you back."

"Yeah, thanks," said Aces.

"What can I do for you?" He yawned and made his way to the kitchen, ready for a beer.

"I'm calling to find out if you know where Gibs is. He was supposed to do some work for me today."

The other eyebrow rose up to meet the one he'd already lifted. He pulled the fridge door open and reached for a bottle. "Really? Doing a side job on your bike?"

"What? No. I wouldn't leech business off you, Spade."

This conversation struck Luke wrong. Gibs, except on rides, usually hung back from the leadership. He couldn't stand the politics. But doing jobs for leadership now? That definitely wasn't his style. Luke had no intention of telling Aces where he'd been all day. "Tell you what. If I hear from him tonight I'll give you a call."

"Great. Thanks."

"Night." Luke hung up on the phone and kicked the fridge door shut with his boot. He didn't know why he held back the information on Gibs, but then, no one had to be involved in Gibs' business either. His employee would have to deal with Aces on his own when he was out of jail.

He twisted off the cap of his Budweiser and sat down on the couch, kicking his feet on top of the coffee table. He dialed Emily. "Hey, babe."

"Hi, Luke. Everything okay now?" Her voice sounded strained though it was obvious she was trying to keep things light.

Luke thought about their conversation regarding her upcoming court case. After what he'd just had to deal with, he figured the last thing she needed to hear about was his employee's incarceration. "It's no big deal. One of my employees did something stupid and didn't want his wife to know."

"Are you an accomplice in his crime now?"

"I suppose. I'm sorry I ran off." Was she teasing him or accusing him? He couldn't seem to tell. He took a long swig of his cold beer.

"That's okay," she said quietly. Her voice was that of a little girl caught doing something wrong.

"Are you all right?" He felt like an idiot asking, but something was up.

"Um, yeah. Look, I gotta go."

And there it was. Emily was pulling away again. Damn, what did he have to do to get her to trust him? "Emily?"

"What Luke?" She sounded exasperated.

He blinked in surprise. Could she be mad at him? "I'll give you a call in a few days."

"That would be best. Goodbye, Luke." She clicked off the line.

Luke just stared at his phone. Her goodbye had the ring of finality as if she didn't want to speak to him anymore. Ever again.

"Fuck!" he said loudly, tossing his phone on the couch and then swiping his bottle off the coffee table.

Shaking his head he guzzled it down. He was pissed off at what was going on about Gibs and letting it spill over into everything else. Everything else, meaning Emily.

Needing a diversion he grabbed his keys and headed out the door to the Red Bull Bar. In a short drive, he was there, bike parked, and heading inside.

Despite it being late on a Monday evening, there was a decent turnout crowd at the Red Bull. It was the hangout of bikers everywhere within a twenty-five-mile radius during the week and almost everyone else on the weekend. Luke walked in and surveyed the floor, making sure none of the Rojos Motor Club were in the room. *Good.* He shrugged off his leather jacket but kept it in his hands. The Red Bull was neutral ground for all riders and everyone was expected to take off their colors before they entered.

Satisfied, he moved to the center of the converted barn where a four-sided bar made of dark wood stood. Glasses of different shapes hung in racks over the bar, and the center island displayed the bar's liquors in tier pyramid. Lights shining from the glass racks illuminated the liquors, their various colors, amber glinting under the harsh light. To the extreme left was a small stage by the wall, but there was no entertainment tonight.

The gray barn board walls were filled with bar pictures, advertisements of beers and liquors. Ancient red leather booths lined the wall in back to the front of the bar. To the right were three pool tables, two of which were occupied. It was a simple place that catered to the blue-collar biker crowd. The most decorative things in the joint were the bras and panties hanging from the rafters, a testament to the nature of its patrons.

John, the brother of the owner, was tending bar tonight, and he nodded at Luke. "What'll it be, Spade?"

"Jack and Coke."

"Oh, moving up in the world," he quipped. Luke didn't usually order mixed drinks.

"It's Monday night. I've work in the morning."

"Anyone from the club in?" John worked many years part-time for his brother and recognized all the frequent customers by club and rank.

"Not tonight."

"And the other club?"

"No Rojos tonight."

"Good."

Luke took one of the red leather bar stools and put his jacket on the one next to him. John set Luke's drink in front of him and

Luke took a sip. He let the liquid slide down his throat and concentrated on shedding the tension in his body. Whatever Gibs was into would work out. And Emily? She did have a lot on her plate with that ridiculous court case. Maybe he was pushing her too hard too fast.

"Easy, guy," he told himself. "You waited for her this long. A little while longer won't kill 'ya."

Yet it didn't feel that way, and thoughts of Emily sliding naked against him manifested more concretely in his faded blue jeans. He took a deep breath and a long sip, letting the liquor and soda burn on its way down. He'd finish this and get home. Sitting here wasn't helping things at all like he hoped it would.

"Luke!" a female voice screeched. "Is that you, Luke Wade?"

He twisted to spot a well-stacked woman with long dark hair bounce toward him. It took a minute to place the face and then it came to him. "Sheila? Sheila Harmon?"

The girl he dated in high school before Emily threw her arms around him and planted a juicy kiss on his cheek. He was sure he'd have to wipe her red lipstick off at the first opportunity.

She pulled away, but still managed to stay near to him. She let her eyes gaze hungrily up and down Luke. She whistled. "Just look at you! You got even better looking!"

"You didn't do so bad yourself," he said with a smile. "What're you doing here?"

"Visiting. Up from Alabama to spend time with the folks. My sister brought me here." She drew out "Alabama" in an exaggerated Southern drawl. "But it's Healey now. Sheila Healey."

"Married?" He glanced down but didn't notice a ring.

She shrugged. "I was. Divorced last year."

"Sorry to hear."

"Don't be. I'm not. And you? Married?"

"Yeah, to a little bike shop called Central Valley Bike Repairs."

"Ah, a man who follows his dreams. I remember you telling me about that."

"You do?"

"Oh, yeah." She poked her finger into his chest and twisted it. "I remember a lot about you, Luke Wade."

"And you? What keeps you in Alabama?"

"My job. I'm a nurse in a hospital." She rolled her eyes. "I don't think they can get along without me."

"I'm sure anyone would find it hard to get along without you," he replied with a smile.

"Mmm, mmm, mmm. That smile." She sighed. "Hey! Let's get together sometime. This weekend maybe?"

"Sorry, I have plans."

"The whole weekend?"

"You caught me at a bad time."

"Well, here." She took a Sharpie out of her purse and wrote a phone number on his hand. "That's my number in town. Give me a call if you find yourself with time on your hands."

"Sure thing, sweetheart."

She broke away and walked to the other side of the bar where her sister waited. But as she did so she looked over her shoulder and gave him a smile.

"Man, that girl's got it bad for you," said John, then he looked over his shoulder. "Oh shit."

Luke heard the door open the same time John did. The look on John's face told him this wasn't going to be good. He didn't bother turning around. Looking at trouble and looking for trouble could sometimes be mistaken for the same thing. He watched John and listened for any signs of warning going on behind him.

He didn't have to wait long.

"Look what we have here. Oooh, a bad Hades' Spawn."

"Move along, Bre," John warned.

"What? The Spawn can't speak for himself?"

Luke stared at his drink, not moving.

A brown hand clasped his shoulder, and instinctively Luke turned on the stool, wrenching the hand away. "Didn't your momma ever teach you to keep your hands to yourself?"

"And didn't your papa teach you that only a *pendejo* snitches."

Luke glared at the asshole spoiling for a fight.

"Boys," said John. "Take it outside."

"I don't know, John. This asshole doesn't have enough self-control to make it outside." Luke was in no mood for a shit-disturber.

"You both know the rules. Drink peaceably, or take it outside." John spoke in a no nonsense tone developed from long years of dealing with bikers.

Luke stood. "No problem, John." He tossed some bills on the bar. "Thanks for the drink. Later." He stood and walked by the Rojos biker. Or at least he tried.

Bre butted his shoulder into Luke's and sneered.

Luke stared at the Rojos. The guy was taller than Luke but thinner.

The Rojos glared at him, his eyes burning for a fight. "Whatcha' going to do, Homes?" said the Rojos.

"I'm going outside. If you dare, come along."

Hate flickered in the Rojos' eyes. He may have started this, but Luke was going to finish it.

"You know the place." Without another glance at the biker, Luke sauntered out of the Red Bull and walked around to the back of the building. Motion sensor floodlights lighted the back as soon as he rounded the corner. The floods spilled light on the blacktop, but the trees and the eight-foot-high picket fence that ran the length of the property were cased in darkness. A dumpster to the right blocked the view of the road that ran perpendicular to the Red Bull. Luke dropped his jacket to the blacktop.

There would be no question in anyone who witnessed the exchange that Luke wasn't going to back out of this. The man had called him not just a dickhead, but also a coward and a snitch, loud enough for everyone in the bar to hear him.

If it were just him, Luke wouldn't have cared as much. But everyone there knew who Luke was and what club he belonged to. While Hades' Spawn wasn't an outlaw club, not one percenters like the Hell's Angel or the Rojos, they had a reputation to uphold. Luke wasn't going to let some skinny asshole from the Rojos smear it for the sake of an old grudge.

Bre followed him to the back and a crowd from the bar followed to watch. They faced each other. Luke sized up the Rojos and waited for the other man to throw the first punch. It was better that way. Luke could get an inkling of how the man fought.

When Luke was in the Navy, he wanted to be a Seal. It sounded exciting and glamorous, and he wanted to join that select cadre of warriors. However, there was too much need for good mechanics and he couldn't get approval to take the training. That didn't stop him from training on his own for the possibility of getting into the program. He swam every morning in the base pool, trained with weights after and took every martial arts class he could. It wasn't Seal training, but it got him into shape and taught him how to fight.

By the way the man stood, Luke knew this man was no trained fighter. At best, he was tried and tested by the violence of his gang, but when it came to one on one, this man didn't know how outmatched he was.

"Come on, asshole," Luke said. "You wanted this."

Chapter Two

Consequences

The Rojos screamed and ran at Luke. Bre held his fists in front of him and swung at him.

Luke turned to one side, and grabbing Bre's shoulders, threw him into the wood privacy fence at the border of the property.

"*Madre*," Bre cursed, standing unsteadily. He brushed his pants with his hands and gave Luke a hard stare.

Luke held up both hands, and with his fingers motioned for the Rojos to come and get him.

The Rojos flew at him again just as gracelessly, but this time as he did so, he pulled a knife from his pocket.

Luke didn't see it until the last moment when it caught the glint of light of the floods. He was going to let the Rojos fly past him again so he'd experience the humiliation of his own incompetence. However, the knife changed the game. He let the man step in and Luke caught him in the throat with an elbow, making him lean back. Swiftly, Luke threw his other elbow into the man's solar plexus, causing him to grunt and drop his knife. He kneed the Rojos in the groin, and Bre stumbled back. Luke laid his hands into the man's face with an uppercut to the jaw and landed successive blows on his face. The satisfaction he wanted to feel didn't come. The fight left him drained, tired and still frustrated. Nothing more.

The Rojos staggered then dropped to the blacktop, his mouth and nose bleeding.

Luke squatted next to him. "Hey, asshole. Had enough?"

Bre gave him a glassy stare and groaned.

"There's a reason why you were told not to bother me, man. That's one. The other is that your *presidente* wants to take a crack at me when he gets out of prison. I know. Not the usual order of things, but I've managed to piss him off good. You won't fuckin' earn your patches by taking me on. There's always one asshole every month or so thinking to make points. Take my advice. Keep your mouth shut. Most likely, if your leadership hears about this, they won't just drum you out; they'd beat you out. Understand?"

The man barely nodded.

"Good." Luke stood and turned to the small crowd that witnessed the fight. He walked toward them after picking up his jacket from the ground to push his way through the crowd.

"Luke! Watch out!"

A searing pain ripped through Luke's thigh. He stumbled and someone held him up. He glanced back to the Rojos, who gave him an ugly grin. Wincing, Luke craned his neck to find a small thin knife sticking out of the back of his thigh.

"Get John," someone called. Others rushed over to the Rojos and held him down.

A few moments later John came out the back door of the Red Bull and stared at the scene. He muttered, but Luke couldn't understand what he said. He pulled out his cell phone.

"Don't," Luke said through gritted teeth.

"It's a knife wound, Spade. It's nothing to fuck with."

"You," shouted John to the Rojos. "Can you walk?"

"Yeah."

"Get the hell outta here then before the police come."

The Rojos got up and staggered toward the parking lot.

"Another thing," John called after him. "Don't come back here. Ever."

A murmur went through the crowd. People were rarely banned from the bar.

Bre spun around and sneered, "Who'd want to come back here?" He merged in the gathering dark as he went to his vehicle.

"And the rest of you get out of here. The bar's closed."

When people lingered. He barked, "Now! No witnesses. Everyone, keep your fucking mouths shut."

The person holding Luke handed him off to John. Luke winced as he hopped on his good leg. Police sirens roared up the highway.

"What're you going to tell them, John?"

"That some idiot attacked you in the parking lot looking to rob you."

"They won't believe that story." He tried to keep his voice low and hide the pain shooting up his leg. He was itching to pull the blade out but knew it could cause more damage than good.

John stared hard at Luke. "Yes, they will if I tell the story. Come on. Let's move into the lot and make this more believable." He helped Luke limp over just as the fire and ambulance pulled in. There were few questions as a paramedic set him on a stretcher prone, and stabilized the knife in his leg.

The police insisted on questioning him at the hospital. He lay on his stomach in the ER bed staring at the walls with his anger simmering. He was waiting for the doctor when the two police officers who had surveyed the initial scene showed up in his hospital room.

"So you really didn't get a look at this guy?" Officer Ignati sounded as if he didn't believe Luke. He stood at the head of the bed on one side, and his partner stood at the head on the other. The guy's partner's face told Luke he didn't believe him either.

Luke couldn't blame either man. "Sorry, officer. My back was turned. I was heading to my bike."

Ignati saw Luke's jacket on the chair. "So this has *nothing* to do with club business."

"We're a social club. Nothing more."

"Because that's an awful funny place to get a wound from a mugging."

"I can't help it if the jerk had poor aim."

"Uh huh. And he got clean away. You didn't do anything to try to get him?"

"Officer, there was a knife in my leg. How was I supposed to run after him?"

"And none of your club was there with you?"

"Nope. Fighting solo tonight."

"*Fighting* solo?" The officer repeated Luke's words, emphasizing the word fighting. "Why's that?"

"I don't spend every minute with the club, officer," growled Luke, getting tired of waiting and lying on his stomach, which he disliked.

"Patience, Mr. Wade. We just have to check these things out. I'm also going to need to look at your driver's license?"

"What the fuck?" Luke knew better to swear, but he was losing patience now.

"Luke? Luke Wade?"

He couldn't place the voice or see who entered the room since his head lay facing away from the door. He tried shifting and grimaced from the pain so he twisted his head, but one of the policemen stood blocking his view.

"Officers. I need to ask Mr. Wade some questions regarding billing before the doctor can see him. So if you don't mind, please wait outside."

The officers looked at each other and walked out of the room.

Luke felt a hand on his good leg. He turned to see a petite lady with longer brown hair dressed in a skirt and blouse. She looked all business and sweet at the same time.

"I'm Angela, Angela Dougherty. Emily's sister." She moved to the head of the bed. "I work in billing. Boy, was I surprised when I saw your name in the computer."

"Hey, Angela." This was not exactly how he wanted to meet Emily's family. First night back with Emily and he drops her off at her place with her parents standing outside her house and now this. "Sorry, I can't get up."

She waved her hand, then set it on her hip. "Does Emily know you are here?"

"No," he said grimly.

"Oh," she said with concern in her voice, and something else. He had no idea how a single word could carry so much meaning. "Okay then, I need your insurance information."

"In my wallet. Back pocket."

"Emily told me you have your own shop."

"Yeah." He wished she didn't have to bring Emily's name up. He didn't want to think about her at this moment.

"And you have insurance?"

"Doesn't everyone have insurance these days?" He tried to make the comment sound light and joking, but it came out sounding sarcastic.

"Yes, of course." Her tone gave nothing away this time.

"I have a business policy for me and my employees."

"Must be expensive." She made a note on the chart she carried.

"Cost of doing business." Was she digging for information or just making conversation? It wasn't a professional remark. Luke felt a tugging at his back pocket, and he winced as his damaged muscles felt as if they were being yanked.

"Sorry," said Angela.

"It's okay," he whispered through gritted teeth.

She handed him his wallet.

He leaned up on his elbows and opened the old black leather worn wallet. "Here's the card."

She took it from him and smiled. "I'll just make a copy. I'll be right back."

He dropped his head down on the pillow and closed his eyes when she left. It had been an incredibly long day. He just wanted the doctor to come in and fix his leg so he could go home. He'd have to take a taxi since his bike was still at the Red Bull.

He heard more footsteps and assumed it was Angela returning. He was wrong.

"Oh, Luke! Are you okay?" Sheila Harmon's voice squealed, her quick heels tapping hurriedly as she moved to the head of the bed.

Luke groaned. "What're you doing here, Sheila?"

"I wanted to check to see if you were okay."

"Don't you remember John saying to get lost?"

"Yeah. But you were hurt."

"Did you check out those police officers out there? They're questioning me, Sheila. You need to leave."

"I won't say anything. Someone has to look after you." She reached over and ran her fingers through his hair to brush it out of his eyes.

More footsteps entered the room. He wished he could see who was coming and going. "Okay, Luke." Angela stopped speaking. "I'm sorry. I didn't mean to interrupt."

Shit! "Angela," Luke said quickly, "you remember Sheila Harmon. She was in my class in high school."

"Yeah," Angela said slowly. "Good to see you, Sheila. Well, everything is set on the insurance side. I'll just put this back in your wallet." She reached for his wallet and fumbled as she tried to stuff his insurance card back inside. She gave up and set the wallet and card on the stand beside his bed. "It's here on the table. See you later, Mr. Wade." Her tone was now professional and clipped.

Luke groaned. Emily would hear about this, including, Sheila Harmon in the room with him.

"Are you okay, Luke?" Sheila asked in a baby voice.

"For shit's sake, Sheila! Can you please leave?" Luke wished he could.

"Fine, Luke." She leaned down and kissed his forehead. "I hope you feel better soon. Call me if you need anything." She grabbed a business card out of her purse and wrote something down on the back before setting it beside his wallet.

"Thanks," he muttered and wiped his face.

Ignati and his partner walked into the room again when Sheila left. Ignati cleared his throat. "We need to ask a couple more questions and then we'll be out of here."

"Sure," said Luke, suppressing a groan. His thigh throbbed painfully, as did his head.

"Your driver's license?"

"Hand me my wallet, please."

The police officer tossed him the wallet. It landed right beside his face on the pillow.

"Here," said Luke, handing him the I.D. card.

Ignati looked at it and wrote some things down on a notepad he took from his pocket, then gave the license back to Luke.

The other guy moved close enough for Luke to read his name badge. Ricci. He needed to remember that. "And you didn't see the man's face?" Ricci asked.

"I didn't see anything."

"Okay," shrugged Ignati. "One of our detectives will contact you."

Really? For a knife wound? Luke bit back the comment. "Okay, officer. Thanks for everything."

Finally the doctor arrived, and the policemen left. The doctor stitched him up and sent him, prescription in hand, on his way. It was nearly seven o'clock in the morning and except for some dozing off here and there, he hadn't slept. But there were things he had to do, and he didn't enjoy the prospect of the long day ahead. He gingerly sat on the bed, thankful for the prescription to numb his leg. He stuffed his wallet and cards in his back pocket.

Saks walked into the room as Luke was trying to put his boots on. "Hey."

"What're you doing here?" Luke blinked in surprise.

"John called. He said you were here." Saks shrugged. "Figured you needed a ride. I came in an hour ago and waited."

"John called you?"

"Little known fact. He's my cousin."

"Uh-huh. Here, give me a hand."

Saks helped Luke put the boot for his injured leg on. "So, what happened?" he asked.

"Some idiot brought a knife to a fist fight."

Saks stared at him before straightening. He waited a moment before crossing his arms over his chest. "You not going to tell me the details then?"

"Best not to." Luke figured the less who knew the details, the better.

"Fine. I'll take you home."

Luke shook his head. "No, take me to the shop and help me get my bike home."

"Yeah, because it's always wise to ignore doctor's orders." Saks rolled his eyes.

Luke hefted his weight onto the crutches the hospital had given him. He grinned. "Yeah. What orders would those be?"

Saks picked up the papers the nurse left Luke on the side table. "The ones that say keep your leg elevated for a couple days and restrict movement."

Luke waved his hand before grasping the handle part of the crutch for support. "Later."

"I'll call Gibs and tell him to open the shop." Saks reached for his phone hanging off his belt.

Shit. "Gibs isn't coming to work today."

"Gibs? Not at work?" Saks' bushy eyebrows rose.

Luke hobbled with the crutches toward the exit, purposely avoiding Saks' question. "Hey, I appreciate you coming down, but we need to make tracks."

"Okay, Boss."

Saks kept glancing at Luke as they drove to the shop. Luke kept his eyes on the road. The morphine they gave to stitch him up had long since worn off and his thigh was throbbing. However, there was shit to do and nothing was going to stop him.

At the shop they switched Saks' car for Luke's SUV and Luke drove it to the Red Bull where Saks loaded Luke's bike on the trailer. They brought it back to the shop and unloaded it in the back. Luke hobbled to his office and printed up what orders and repairs needed to be done today. He handed it to Saks. "You're in charge. Text if you need me."

Luke crawled back in the SUV, his jaw clenched from the pain in his leg. It was eight thirty in the morning now, and Luke wanted to get a shower and some clean clothes. Getting up the stairs to his apartment on crutches was strenuous, and by the time he was in his apartment the only thing he wanted was to put the throbbing leg up. He swallowed two of the pain pills the doctor had prescribed at the same time. Foregoing a shower, he cleaned up the best he could, dressed, and made a makeshift ice pack from ice in his fridge. He put the ice pack under his leg as he drove to the Superior Courthouse in Middletown.

Getting down from the SUV was as much an adventure on the crutches as waiting in line at the courthouse to get in. Irritated, he sighed and leaned his weight on the props under his armpits, trying to give his sore leg some reprieve. He had left his colors at home, just to avoid aggravation, but he needed to go through the metal detector. Seeing him on crutches the officers manning the detectors waved him over and ran the wand over him.

"Where can I find out what's on the docket?" asked Luke.

An officer pointed to a kiosk on the left side of the hall. Luke hobbled over and looked over the docket. His mouth dropped when he found Gibs.

Gibson, Francis, Possession of Controlled Substance/Intent to Sell

Anger began to boil in Luke's gut. This shit *again*? Didn't the club have enough to live down with Okie in prison? He didn't know what the hell was going on, but he intended to find out. Gibs had a lot to explain. A hell of a lot.

Luke's cell phone buzzed in his pocket. He reached for it and flipped it on. "What?" he growled.

"Luke?" It was Helen, Gibs' wife. She sounded worried. "Have you seen Gibs? He didn't come home last night."

"Um, sorry Helen." He lowered his voice and tried to sound apologetic. He wasn't sure what to tell her. He ran a few scenarios in his head, before finally answering. "I had a little accident and I've been in the Emergency Room the entire night. He's here now squaring away a few things."

"Oh, okay." The relief in her voice made him feel incredibly guilty. "What an idiot. He should have called."

"Yes," agreed Luke. "He should have."

"Tell him to call when he gets a chance."

"I will." He hated lying to Helen, but it wasn't his place to tell her what was going on. That was Gibs' job.

The doors to the courtroom opened and because of his injury, the guard let him through first. Luke hobbled in with everyone else after him to wait.

Chapter Three

The Warning

The dark circles under Emily's eyes bore witness to her sleepless night. She had given up on actually sleeping long before the sun had risen. She'd tossed and turned in bed, unable to get her brain to relax and stop trying to overthink everything regarding Luke. In the wee hours of the night, her mind had gone from terrible outcomes to the worst imaginable.

On one hand, what Angela said was entirely correct. Emily couldn't afford to get into any more trouble by dating someone who was associated with criminals. On the other, the words Luke spoke to her the last time she was with him rang in her ears.

"Emily, you seriously going to tell me that you're going to let bullshit like this get in the way of us?"

She turned the alarm off way before it was set to go off, made her bed, fed Reger, and took a shower mechanically. She moved through her apartment as if all life had drained from her. The anger and desolation she experienced that summer when her parents forbade her to see Luke filled her once more. It was like a funeral. Like losing someone close to her and she felt lost.

That same sense of failure engulfed her. Once again, circumstances spun out of her control. What was she supposed to do? Deny her love for him once again and walk away? Should she jeopardize her future because an idiot ex-boyfriend threw every obstacle in her way? Was fate having a laugh at her again? Or was this punishment for—

Her cell phone rang, interrupting her thoughts.

"Hi, Emily. It's Justin."

"Hey, Justin." She tried to sound composed but heard the depression in her own voice.

"Evan just called. He's willing to sign the car over to you if you pay off the rest of the loan."

What? Freakin' bullcrap! Evan could kiss her butt. "No!" She preferred the anger in her voice now over the pathetic wimp a second ago.

"No?"

"He took it. Let him deal with it."

"He did say he'd drop the charges."

"So? How's that going to help? Does it make up for what he's put me through so far? This is not my fault. None of it is."

"Maybe you shouldn't look at it that way."

"Whose lawyer are you, Justin?" She turned her annoyance to him. "I don't trust anything he says. Let's be realistic here. He's not finished with me." She shook her head, Evan was a nut job. "I gave you proof of every payment I made. He can't dispute that."

"Maybe." Justin sighed. "If it was just that Theft charge, yeah. But then there is the Reckless Endangerment charge. The more we can get knocked off before we go back, the easier it'll be to get the rest of the charges reduced. A Reckless charge won't just impact your sentence, it could impact whether or not you'll keep your license. It'll make your insurance payments go up as well. The speeding charge doesn't help either." What were you thinking?

He didn't ask the question but Emily was sure he had said it in his head.

She wanted to swear. Her entire life she was the good girl. Then, just because she wanted out of a relationship going nowhere, and for fifteen minutes of poor judgment on the road, she was screwed. It wasn't fair. She wanted to scream and rip her hair out. Rrrgghh!

"So what do you say, Em? Do you want to take Evan's offer?"

Emily sighed. "I'll think about it. I don't have the money to pay off the car, but I'll try and see if I can get a loan."

"Maybe your dad—"

"No! Certainly not." She had no intention of asking them for anything or dragging them further into the Evan-fiasco.

"All right. Just a suggestion."

She checked the clock on the wall. "I've got to get to work, Justin."

"Think about it, Emily. I'll talk to you later."

"Thanks. For everything. I do appreciate your help." Guilt had her apologizing for snapping at him.

"Hey, we're practically family," he said, his voice softening and losing the lawyer tone. "If I don't talk to you sooner, I'll see you at Sunday dinner. Call me with your decision." He clicked off.

Emily swallowed hard. Now that her parents were back from Florida, they'd expect her to go to dinner at their house on Sunday. She wasn't looking forward to it, not after the way she yelled at them. Whether she was wrong or right, she'd have to apologize for raising her voice at them. And she'd have to apologize to her mother for making her cry.

It was the right thing to do even though her mother made her cry plenty of times. The bitterness of her teenage years and the control her father still had over her ate at her heart. She was young when she fell in love with Luke back then, but it was love. The connection they shared was pure and sweet. Her parents didn't understand. They only saw a leather jacket and a motorbike. They still thought the same way today. Evan had the proper haircut, the right family background, everything. They couldn't see the real picture.

An image of Luke popped into her head. He was even more handsome now than he was as a teenager. She realized something else. Now that they made love, Emily knew she was falling for him again. She was falling in love with him. The memory of his hard body against hers, the smell of him and the hungry way he touched her made her shiver. There was no mistaking the want and need she had for that luscious man.

Needing to clear her head, she picked up her purse and made her way outside. After locking the door, she hurried to her sister's car to get to work. Daydreams didn't pay the rent. She climbed in and pushed away her thoughts of Luke Wade. At least she tried to.

Emily cursed looking at the clock on the dashboard of the car. The glut of cars on the highway choked a swift ride into New Haven as everyone moved at a slow crawl. The last thing she needed was to be late again. Her employers were rapidly losing patience with her tardiness and absences. Five years of hard work were rapidly wasting under one month of hard luck and bad choices.

Slapping her hand on the signal arm she glanced over her shoulder to scan her chances of pulling over in the extreme right-hand lane. Typical of New Haven drivers, cars passed her on the right anyway. They ignored her signal light and weren't willing to let her in. Except she had to get to that lane. If she took the next exit she'd have a chance of getting to work on time.

Heart pounding, she stuck the nose of the car in the first small space of an opening when the car ahead on the right-hand side pulled away. The car in back of her honked and kept sounding the horn as Emily wedged her way into the lane. *Sorry, Horn Honker.*

Emily's hands shook. She had never managed a move like that before. She didn't know whether to be triumphant she pulled it off or scared shitless she was that stupid. But she was in the lane, and when the exit came up she dashed down it. The minutes ticked away as she navigated the local traffic and streetlights to get to her job. It seemed to take forever.

Finally, she arrived in the parking lot. The clock let her know she had five minutes to spare. Counting that a minor miracle, she got out of her car.

And stopped short.

"Hi, Baby."

Emily's heart pounded at an erratic rate. She knew the voice; did not want to talk to him. She turned slowly.

Evan stood leaning against his car. "I've been waiting to talk to you. You're late."

Emily straightened; resolved not to speak a word to him. She avoided meeting his gaze and walked past him.

Except Evan wasn't going to allow that. He grabbed her arm and jerked her to face him. "Hey. I said I wanted to talk to you."

"I'm late," said Emily coldly.

"Be late," he said. "I hate how you are avoiding me."

"Too bad." She yanked her arm from his grasp.

Quickly he moved to block her path.

"Get out of my way," growled Emily. Why couldn't someone walk by to see this altercation going on? At least she'd have some proof to his craziness.

"Not until you talk to me."

Emily crossed her arms. He wasn't going to leave her alone until he told her what he wanted to say. "About what?"

"I want you back." He smiled.

She took a deep breath as her stomach rolled. She couldn't believe him. "Why would you want a slut?"

"I'm sorry, Emily. I lost my temper." He didn't look remorseful at all.

"You seemed perfectly calm to me when you said it."

"Things haven't been going right for me since I lost my job. Losing you was the last straw. I promise, Em, if you take me back I'll change. I'll give you the car back, and I'll stop drinking. I swear Emily. Please."

Could Evan change? She wasn't sure if she cared if he did. He'd gone too far and done too much damage. She'd never trust him again. Her watch beeped. She sighed. "Evan, I can't talk now.

If I don't get in that building right now, we'll both be out of jobs."

"Then you'll talk to me later?"

"I've got to go," she said firmly. She tried to maneuver around Evan, but he wouldn't budge. "Please, Evan."

"Give me a kiss." He pressed his lips together and closed his eyes...

"What?" she screeched. "Get out of my way right now!"

Evan grabbed her arm again, and she twisted, trying to get away from him.

"Is there a problem here?" The building's security guard strode toward them.

Evan instantly let go of her arm. "No problem," he said quickly. "I'll call you later, Em." He got into his car and peeled out of the driveway.

"Are you okay, Miss?" asked the guard.

"I've told him to leave me alone. And he just won't." Her shaking hands returned.

"Yeah. Assholes don't seem to remember that," said the guard. He shook his head. "I'll walk you in."

"You don't have to," she said but appreciated his gesture.

"It's my job. Don't take it personally." He winked at her. He was an older man, dressed in a white uniform shirt and black pants. The guard gazed at her with a fatherly expression on his face.

"Sure. Is it okay if you don't walk in my office with me, please? I don't want the people there talking."

"Okay. I can do that."

Emily found her knees unsteady and thought she was going to lose her breakfast. Only, she realized, she was so upset she hadn't had breakfast this morning.

"This is turning out to be a stellar morning," she mumbled under her breath when the guard left her at the elevator. She managed to make it to her desk in one piece without falling apart.

"Emily!"

Before she could sink her nerve-wracked body in her chair, her boss, Eric Hobson, motioned for her to come into his office.

Swallowing, she entered his office where he sat behind his broad desk. Hobson was in his mid-thirties, an up and comer in the financial side of their company's business. He seemed to work in the office twenty-four seven. At least, he was always in before she arrived and when she left each day.

"Don't shut the door. Please sit down, Emily," he said seriously.

Emily took the chair in front of his desk, her heart racing.

"You're late again, Emily. Is there a reason?"

Emily wanted to cry. She should have had the guard walk her in. "The traffic was bad," she said weakly.

"Bad traffic is not news here, Emily. You should plan your morning better."

"Yes, sir."

"You've been late an unacceptable number of days this month, Emily, and you've missed others. This can't continue."

"I understand, Mr. Hobson." Emily stared down at her hands, blinking to hold back the tears. It was like a nightmare just getting worse and worse. She slowly looked up when he didn't say anything else.

He seemed to have relaxed and leaned back in his chair. "Are there problems of which I should be aware?"

"No, sir." She knew better than to discuss her personal problems with her boss.

"You've been a very good employee up to now, Emily, which is why I've been lenient with you. But the other employees are beginning to talk, and I can't have that."

"Talk?" said Emily, confused.

"Favoritism," he said. "They think I show you favoritism and are coming up with creative reasons as to why."

Emily's mouth dropped open. "They don't think—" Her face burned red as she couldn't finish her sentence.

He nodded. "Yes, they do. And it's bad when employees think that. Considering your recent attendance record, I've no choice but to issue you a written warning."

Tears stung Emily's eyes, which she fought back furiously. She'd have been at her desk on time if it weren't for Evan. Damn it! This wasn't her fault! Morons talking around the water cooler was the problem here. "I understand, Mr. Hobson," said Emily as bile rose in her stomach.

He pulled out a piece of paper and placed it in front of her. "Please read it now. Out loud."

Seriously? She looked at him to see if he was joking. He wasn't.

So Emily read the document,

"Emily Dougherty

Junior Account

RE: Written Warning for Attendance

Miss Emily Dougherty,

This letter is to serve as an official written reprimand for an incident that happened on this date. As per policy, you were not at your desk and ready to work at 9:00 AM.

This is not the first time that we have had this issue with you being tardy. Absenteeism and lateness have been a problem in the recent past and it appears verbal counseling has not been effective.

On April 6 and again on April 13 you did not report for work, and you were late on three other occasions this month. On April 21 we discussed these issues, at which time I issued a verbal warning to you regarding your attendance.

We value attendance and consider it to be a significant factor in your position. It is essential to the efficient operation of our office that every employee be ready to perform their duties in a timely manner. Repeated lateness and absences have a corrosive effect on office morale as it often forces other employees to do the work assigned to you. This is a disservice to the employees who are covering for you. Proper attendance and being on time is necessary for the overall functioning of our company.

We value your contributions to the enterprise. Consequently, we see this as a step to inform you of the seriousness with which we consider this matter and give you an opportunity to correct your performance.

Failure to arrive on time at work or further unapproved absences may result in further disciplinary procedures up to and including termination.

Please refer to the Progressive Discipline section of your Employee Handbook for more information on disciplinary procedures or contact Human Resources if you have questions. Otherwise, my door is always open to discuss particular problems that may impede your ability to arrive on time or attend when you are scheduled.

Please sign and date below. A copy will be placed in your personnel file. Signing does not indicate that you agree with this warning, only that we discussed it.

Sincerely,

Eric Hobson

Manager, Accounting Department."

Emily quickly signed the letter with shaking hands even as her stomach turned cold. She handed it to him, not even sure she remembered a word of what she had just read. Her head spun. "Is there anything else, Mr. Hobson?"

"No, Emily." His phone rang and he turned in his swivel chair after picking up the handset.

Emily made it to her desk but didn't know how. She put her face in her hands. If she didn't get this nonsense under control, she was going to lose her job and everything she had worked for.

Chapter Four

Felonies

A bunch of misdemeanor cases came and went first. These had
lawyers who wanted to do their business and get out of the
courthouse. Luke half listened to the nonsense about people
picked up on minor theft charges, domestic violence cases, and
similar things. His leg grew more painful as the minutes ticked
by. The room was packed so he couldn't put his leg up and
people walking by jostled it if he stuck it out.

By the time they called out the prisoners, Luke was in intense
pain and ticked off. Gibs glanced around the room as he shuffled
in shackles. He caught Luke's eye and Luke did his best to smile.
Except now Luke was incensed. Gibs wouldn't hurt anyone and
seeing him chained made him angry.

The charges were read against Gibs.

"Do you have an attorney, Mr. Gibson?" said the Judge.

"No."

"I suggest you get one. If you cannot, the court will appoint
one for you. The charges against you carry significant jail time. In
the meantime, I'll enter a plea of not guilty until we can come
back to court. Are you employed, Mr. Gibson?"

"Yes."

"For how long?"

"Five years."

"I see. And you don't have a prior record. However, due to the
severity of the charges against you, I'm ordering a fifty-thousand-
dollar bond. Your family or friends can pay the entire amount at
the clerk of court, or you can employ a bondsman who'll handle
the transaction. In the meantime, Mr. Gibson, stay out of

trouble. Be back in court on," he looked at his clerk who mouthed a date, "May Sixteenth. Next case."

Gibs, whose face blanched to a sickly white, glanced at Luke as the sheriff led him away. Luke nodded, hoping Gibs understood it to mean that he'd take care of things.

It took him a couple hours to arrange for a bail bondsman. In the end, he had to put up the title for all three of his bikes plus his SUV and hand over five thousand dollars to secure the bond.

The bail bondsman, Ronaldo, was a tall, heavily built man who looked like he could stop a Mack truck by yanking on it. He was amiable and patient with Luke's questions. Luke thought the bail was very high for a first offense.

"Yeah," agreed Ronaldo. "With almost everything else, except violent crime, you can get released on a promise to appear. But with drug cases the courts are hardcore. I'm not a lawyer, but if he had one at the hearing the lawyer could have argued to lower the bond. The best thing for your friend to do is get a lawyer and get the bond reduced. That way I can release the titles on some of your property."

"It's not like I'm going to sell any of them."

"I hear ya. Nice bikes. I'd like one of them myself. Okay, I'll go to the courthouse now and get that set for you. You should be able to pick up your friend in a couple hours. He's probably still in the holding cells in the courthouse, so you'll have to wait until they take him back to the police department. I'll call over to Westfield and let them know the bond is put up so they don't transfer him to a state facility."

"They'd do that?" Luke shook his head, shock numbing his pain a moment.

"They don't hold people long-term in the local jails."

Luke sucked in a sharp breath. They would move Gibs? The guy wouldn't last a day in a state facility. The pain in his leg returned, along with a headache born of tension. After dealing with the bail bondsman, Luke was in a bad mood when he picked

Gibs up from the Westfield Police Department. It was nearly five o'clock and Helen had called a couple times looking for Gibs. He was too furious to talk or even ask Gibs what the hell was going on. He knew if he said anything, he'd blow his top.

Gibs didn't seem to notice Luke's mood. Probably too happy to be out of the slammer. "Hey!" Gibs pointed down at Luke. "What's with the crutches?"

Luke just shook his head and started for the parking lot. "I'll tell you later. I'm in no mood to discuss it right now. I'll drop you home so you can deal with your wife, and figure out where you are going to get the five thousand dollars I had to give to the bail bondsman." *Not to mention everything else I just put up to cover your ass.* "I'm going to want an explanation for this horseshit going on, but not today. Not bloody today."

"Yeah, that was one hell of a bail, eh? Don't worry. I've got some money put away."

Luke stopped walking and turned to stare at his employee. "I can't believe you're this calm, Gibs."

"I'm not. It's hidden under the beard."

Luke grunted as he climbed into the SUV. Gibs took Luke's crutches and put them in the center between him and Luke.

"Man, what did you do to yourself?" Gibs said as he strapped himself into his seat and watched Luke try to sit with his leg half propped on the towel that had once covered the now melted ice bag on the floor.

"Worry about your own problems, Gibs. You got enough on your plate." Luke started the SUV and glared at Gibs.

"Hey, throw me a bone here! You probably told Helen you've been with me all day, and I have to give her a story."

"You deal with your wife your own way, but I suggest, seeing the amount of money this is costing, you tell her the truth."

"Yeah," said Gibs glumly, slumping in his seat. "You're probably right."

Both men fell into silence after that and until they reached Gibs' house in a tidy suburban area of Westfield. The houses here were modest, but nicely kept. It was a working man's neighborhood, where small fishing boats took up residence in the driveways of their owners.

"I'll get you the money," said Gibs as he got out of the SUV. "I promise."

"I know you will," said Luke, trying to smile. "I know where you work."

Gibs gave him a grin and shut the door. "See you tomorrow, bright and early."

Luke nodded and drove away. He didn't know what to think or even how to respond to Gibs' situation. He was tired from the lack of sleep and the long day. He needed some food, a couple of cold drinks and his bed.

He groaned when he pulled into his parking lot and saw Sheila Harmon leaning against a car. The last thing he needed was this. He had stopped to pick up the full prescription of his painkillers and first aid supplies. He had planned to pick up pizza but had been too tired and figured he'd order delivery. Now fending off Sheila was not on his to-do list tonight.

"Hi, Luke!" She smiled.

He lurched forward on the crutches. His bag from the pharmacy with bandages, tape and pain meds rustled against the crutches. "How'd you find my place?"

"I checked at your shop, but Tony told me you were home. I came by to see if you needed anything. He told me you're supposed to keep the leg up." She tutted and shook her head, purposely trying to get her hair to sway with it.

Saks gave her his address? Traitor. Luke would talk to him later. "I had to pick up a few things from the pharmacy."

"Now, see." She smiled slyly. "That's where I can be useful."

"I'm all right, Sheila. I'm only supposed to be on crutches for a couple days."

"Yeah, and that big dark spot of blood on the back of your jeans tells me that ain't happening. Let's get you upstairs and I'll take a look at it."

Luke gave her a disparaging look.

"I'm a registered nurse, for Pete's sake, Luke! And I can tell by looking at you that you haven't followed doctor's orders. If you don't want to be in the emergency room again tonight, you'll let me help you."

Sobered by Sheila's warning, Luke allowed her to help him up the stairs.

"Get in the bedroom and drop those pants," she ordered in a no-nonsense tone. "Where's your towels?"

Luke pointed at a closet by the bathroom door. He went into his bedroom and after fishing out his phone from his front pocket, he undid his belt. His jeans dropped but stuck to the bandage at the back of his thigh. Luke stood in his boxers with his back to the door. Behind him, he heard Sheila sigh.

"Men! You think you don't have to listen to anyone."

Luke turned his head to look at her. "Believe me, I had important business. Otherwise, I would have been resting today."

"There's nothing more important than your health." She knelt behind him and carefully peeled back his jeans off the bandage.

"Yup. It's oozing pretty good. You need that bandage changed."

He turned to face forward again, embarrassed. "I'll take care of it."

"And how'll you do that? You enjoyed playing Twister in high school, but no amount of pretzel movements will allow you to get to that wound."

"The only reason I played Twister was to get close to the girls."

She yanked on the bandage and pulled down.

"Yow!" Burning pain shot through his leg and burned deep in his gut. He lost his breath for a split second.

"Of course you did. Why do you think I let you play Twister with me?" She teasingly swatted the back of his head and then pointed at his bed. "Lay down on your front."

He lowered himself onto his unmade bed. Face down in his pillows he caught a faint whiff of Emily's scent. He hadn't changed the sheets for that very reason, though he supposed he should eventually change them.

She tutted again. "I'm going to wash it with some soap and water, and check the bleeding. You need to stay off the leg just as the doctor said. Stab wounds aren't sutured shut, so you have to reduce movement and let the wound scab over." She did sound like a nurse. A smart one.

"Okay, okay," groused Luke.

"It's going to be uncomfortable while I do this. From your muscles and build, I'm sure you can handle it."

"Yeah. That's how the day has gone." He ignored her last comment.

Sheila cleaned the wound, being very gentle. Still as she hit sore spots, he winced. She put a fresh, large square bandage over the wound and taped it down with perfect precision. He couldn't see it, but he could tell from the comfortable pressure on the back of his leg.

"You can turn over now," Sheila said and left the room.

Luke turned and grunted, kicking his jeans off of his good leg. He needed new pants that were clean. He'd rather just stay in his boxers.

Sheila returned with a glass of water.

"I'd prefer a beer," he said.

She shrugged. "Your choice. A beer or the painkillers. You can't have both."

He rolled his eyes as he sat up. "Spoken like a member of the medical profession. Fine, I'll take the painkillers."

She fished out the bottle from the bag from the pharmacy and handed him a pill.

"Just one?" he said.

"One every six to eight hours. The other pills are the antibiotics you need to take with food. Trust me, these pain pills are strong enough. They aren't anything to fool with. Wait till the funky dreams start." She laughed.

"I'll take your word on it. Do you mind grabbing me the pair of pants on top of the dresser you are standing beside?"

She sat on the edge of the bed close to him. "Are you sure you want me to do that?"

"Yes." He swallowed, aware of her closeness and his inability to shift smoothly away.

"Hmm. I think you're lightheaded from pushing yourself too much."

"I need food. I was going to order a pizza."

She rolled her eyes. "Of course. The go-to food for guys everywhere."

Luke swiped his phone off the nightstand. With a push of a button he was connected to Jimmi's Pizza. "Are you making deliveries tonight? Good. I'll take a large pepperoni and sausage. Yep." He pointed to his pants on the floor and Sheila, eyebrows raised, handed them to him. He fished out his wallet and gave his card number to the guy on the phone. "One last thing, can you throw in a bottle of Coke? Great." He clicked off the phone and looked up at Sheila sitting on the edge of his bed. "It'll be here in thirty minutes."

"Perfect timing for delivery." She leaned over and pressed her lips to his.

Her lips were sweet and sexy, but she was not what he wanted. He gently pushed her away. "I'm seeing someone."

She put her hand on his good thigh, scrapping her nails with perfect pressure against his bare skin. "I don't see her here now."

"She's working." He swallowed, annoyed his body was responding to her closeness when his head wasn't.

"Well, she's not here, and I'm only in town for a few days. You know, Luke, I always had a thing for you."

He tried to lean back more, but she quickly filled the space. "Sheila, you helped me, and I appreciate that, but I'm really into this woman."

Sheila huffed and then sat up straight and looked away. "You know, there are people you don't, can't forget. And for me, Luke, that was you. But I guess you can't go backwards." She sighed. "Do you mind if I hang around for pizza?"

"Not if you let me put my pants on." He grinned.

She smiled back at him. "I guess we have a deal then." She glanced down at his hard-on still pressing against his boxers. "Too bad." She put her index finger in her mouth and slowly brought her eyes to his as she sucked on her finger. "Really too bad," she whispered.

Chapter Five

The Arrest

Emily tried her best to get her work done, but the warning she received in the morning totally wrecked her day. As soon as it came time to leave work she was beyond ready for it to be the end of the day. She couldn't stop feeling tired and wrung out. When she stepped out the door, the security guard from the morning strode over to her.

"Let me walk you to your car," he said.

"I should be okay."

"It wasn't a question." His stern face softened. "Listen, Miss; I saw how that guy was hassling you this morning. You shouldn't take it lightly. Guys like that don't quit." He crossed his arms over his chest. "I want to make sure you are safe in your car."

Emily nodded, grateful this stranger took the time to make sure she was safe in the short term. She only wished she could be assured of the long-term. She had a feeling he was right about Evan. The guy wasn't going to quit. The only problem was that she couldn't do anything about it. The police believed she was the one harassing him like a crazy ex.

"Thanks so much," she said to the guard as she unlocked the car door and slipped inside. As she waited for him to walk back to the building, she plugged in her phone to the car jack and put on the headset. Her sister usually called after she woke up from her third shift job at the local hospital. Angela was consistent and Emily appreciated it.

Almost as soon as she pulled into the heavy afternoon traffic of I-91 her phone chimed.

"Hey," said Angela.

"Hi. You sound tired. You sleep all right?" Emily felt sorry for her sister. The girl worked nonstop.

"I'm fine. How was your day?"

"Awful. Just horrible." Emily inhaled, needing the air to explain the shit that had hit the fan that day. "Evan showed up outside work and wouldn't leave. The dickhead made me late to work."

"What an idiot."

"I tried to tell him to get lost, he wouldn't leave. The guard for the building came and then Evan finally left. The guard walked me inside. It was so embarrassing."

"That sucks, but it's not the end of the world."

The eternal optimist. "Wait, it gets better. Since he made me late, Mr. Hobson gave me a written warning, and had me read it out loud in his office. It was brutal."

"Oh, I'm so sorry. That really does suck." Angela hesitated on the phone before adding, "Did you call Justin?"

"No. That was the last thing on my mind after I got the warning."

"You'd better call him. If Evan's messing things up for you at work, then you have to report him stalking you."

"I know." Emily sighed. "It's just not going to work. Evan's going to turn it around and make it look like I'm the one stalking him."

"At your workplace? I don't think so. You also have the guard to back your story up."

"I guess." Emily wasn't convinced.

"We'll come over tonight. You can tell Justin what happened. We'll do dinner or something."

"To be honest, Angela, I'm all worn out. I wouldn't be good company."

"Is that the truth?"

"Pardon?" Emily raised her eyebrows and checked her blind spot to see if she could switch lanes. "What do you mean by that?" Her sister probably figured she was going to go and stalk Evan at his house instead. With the way her day was going, she might as well.

"You're not planning on going to see Luke, are you?"

So that was the reason. "No. I told him we needed to cool it for a while." She hesitated to tell her sister why. It didn't seem like a bad idea. She pictured his handsome smile and going for a ride on his bike. It felt a lot more promising than the evening she had planned.

"I'm glad. He's trouble, Em."

"That's what Mom and Dad keep saying."

"No, I saw him."

That caught her attention.

"Where?"

"At the hospital."

"Was he visiting someone?"

"No. He got into a knife fight last night."

"What! How do you know?"

"Professionally, I shouldn't say anything. And don't you dare tell anyone I told you. It would mean my job if anyone found out that I gave out information on a patient."

"I wouldn't ever say anything, Angela. You know that." She had images of poor Luke bludgeoned near to death. Evan probably had paid some guy to do it. "What happened?" Her heart raced and she swore every goosebump on her arms had just risen.

"I don't know the exact details. But cops were questioning him and waiting around to ask him more stuff. He wasn't alone, Em. I'm sorry."

"What do you mean?"

"Sheila Harmon was there at the hospital with him."

"Sheila? From high school Sheila?" She pulled out into the passing lane and then quickly tried to edge back into the middle lane before the car in front blocked her.

"Yeah."

"I thought she moved away." The horn behind her honked so she waved and mouthed *Sorry!* in the rearview mirror.

"Apparently not. It was her all right."

It was too much. The incidents with Evan and the warning letter were bad enough. Had the phone even had time to get cold after their last phone conversation before Luke hooked up with another woman? Maybe he was already seeing her. She had no idea. Luke could be dating ten women and screwing another fifty. She had no clue. Nor had she bothered to ask or pay attention. Her heart sunk deep into her stomach. She opened the window, suddenly finding it hard to breathe. "I've got to go."

"I'm so sorry, Em. Are you okay?"

"I'm fine," she lied. "I just have to concentrate on the traffic. The last thing I need is an accident."

"You sure?"

The car behind honked again. This time trying to tell her to start rolling forward before losing the space in front of her to another idiot driver. "It's busy today. Crazier than usual."

"Sounds like it. Okay, I'll talk to you later. Drive safe."

The phone clicked off and Emily was left with her thoughts as she traveled the highway. Here she was, in the middle lane of the three-lane highway with a car ahead of her, loads behind and cars on either side, but she was utterly alone. She felt as if she was hanging by a thread, as if the earth was opening at her feet, threatening to drag her into the darkness below. It was a shitty, shitty day.

Her hands began to shake. She gripped the wheel of the car so tight her knuckles turned white. She fought back her tears because she couldn't drive if she cried and she wanted to get home so very badly. She planned to crawl into her bed and forget this day had ever happened. Maybe she'd never come out of her room again.

Finally, after what seemed like forever, she made it to her exit
and got off the highway. Rush hour traffic clogged the secondary
roads, and she inched forward in stop and go traffic. She drove in
a daze, images of Luke with other women popping into her head
and making everything so complicated. Shiela Harmon? Really?

Emily made it to her street and breathed a sigh of relief.

It was premature.

Her friggin' car was sitting in front her house! Parked
perfectly in her spot and looking shined and polished.

"Shit Evan!" she muttered. "What're you up to now?" She
knew better than to face him alone after this morning. She pulled
over to the curb at a house three houses away from hers and
called Justin. "Come on, come on," she whispered.

"Hello?" said Justin.

"Thank goodness! It's me, Justin!" In her panic she rushed her
words. "Evan won't leave me alone! He was waiting for me
outside my work this morning, and now my car's sitting in front
of my house! What if he's inside? What if he's going through my
stuff?" Her voice rose in near hysteria at the thought.

"Where are you?"

"Parked at the curb three houses away from mine."

"Do you see him?"

"No."

"Stay there. Don't move. I'm coming over now. Lock your car
doors and whatever happens do not open them for Evan."

"I'm not going anywhere." *Hurry, please!* she added silently.

She swallowed hard as Justin clicked off the call. What was
she supposed to do while she waited? She shrugged down in her
seat and reached for her phone, checking her messages absently,
not focusing on any one message. Maybe Luke sent a text to
explain things. Maybe it was a misunderstanding and he wanted
to tell her why Sheila Harmon was there taking care of him at the
hospital.

Nope. Nothing. Of course not. He'd abandoned her and why wouldn't he? There were plenty of other women who'd want him; plenty of others who wouldn't push him away. Or had a disastrous life and family he didn't have to deal with.

A hard rap on the window made her jump and her phone slipped out of her hand. She turned her head to see Evan standing at the side of the car.

"Emily!" He frowned at her. "What're you doing parked here, so far from your house?"

"Go away, Evan!" she shouted.

He blinked in surprise. "Come on out, Ems. I just want to talk to you."

"I don't wish to speak to you."

Evan reached for the door handle, and Emily banged the door lock shut as fast as she could. Her erratic heart rate pounded against the inside of her head and rang in her ears. What if he turned furious and tried to break the window? She shivered at the thought.

"Emily, be reasonable. I brought your car back."

"Really? Why would you do that! So you can call the police on me the next time I drive it?"

"Emily. I'm sorry. I was stupid."

"You got that right!"

"Damn it! Open the door, Emily," he snapped. He put his hands on the top of the door and leaned down to press his face into the window. "Get. Out. Now. Bitch!"

Emily shrank away.

Evan's mouth drew into a tight line as he clenched his jaw. His storm-filled eyes frightened her more than anything else ever had in her life.

"Go away, Evan! Leave me alone!" Emily trembled as she reached for her phone that had fallen at her feet. It lay halfway between the seat and the console. Her long fingers felt the phone case and just as she managed to curl them around to pull it forward, Evan slapped the window with his hand so hard, she jumped and lost the phone again.

"Emily, open the fucking door right now!"

Terrified, she shook her head frantically, reaching for the phone again and begging that she could get it before he shattered the glass all over her. Finally, her fingers found the phone and she pushed it toward her legs so she could grab it.

If the car ride home had felt long, this simple task seemed to take forever. The smooth case slid suddenly toward her feet and she quickly reached down to grab it. "See this?" she hissed, her hands shaking so bad she had to clutch at the phone to prevent it from flying out of her hand again. "If you don't go away, now, I'm going to call 911. I'll get the police here, Evan."

"Do that," he said with venom in his voice and pure hatred in his eyes, "and you'll be sorry! Incredibly sorry."

Despite the fact Emily hadn't called the police yet, a Walkerville police cruiser pulled up next to them, lights flashing. For once, something had gone her way today.

Evan's face tightened in pure rage. "You stupid bitch!" he yelled.

The police officer got out of his car but remained at the driver's side of the cruiser. "Sir, on the ground with hands on your head."

Evan turned to Emily before he kneeled down. He mouthed the words, "You're gonna be fuckin' sorry!"

She had no doubt she would be.

He was a monster with the face of an angel. Or he tried to look like an angel. Only now, all Emily saw was a demon.

Another police car pulled up and parked in back of Emily. Justin and Angela arrived behind it and parked in back of it. Soon Emily's neighbors were sticking their heads out the doors or standing on their porch watching the spectacle of two police cruisers in the street, Evan, and Emily.

One officer was talking to Evan, who was standing now and talking with his arms crossed.

"Miss, please get out of the car," said the second officer.

Emily unlocked the car and stepped out. The officer asked her name and to see her driver's license and he filled out information in his notebook.

"What's the problem?" said the officer as he handed her the driver's license.

"I've told him to leave me alone. He won't. He was at my work this morning and made me late, so I was given a written warning. Then he showed up here." She knew she was babbling because of shock, but couldn't stop herself. She sounded like a moron complaining about the written warning. Her cheeks flamed with embarrassment.

The police officer didn't appear to notice. "Then, you didn't ask him here?"

"No! Never! Not after what happened."

Justin hurried over. "I'm Emily's lawyer, officer, Justin Kennedy." He handed the police officer his card. "What's going on?"

"The neighbors called in a disturbance."

"Emily called me as soon as she saw Mr. Waters' car in her driveway. Per my instructions she stayed in her car until I could get here."

"Is that right, Miss?"

"Yes." Her head bobbled up and down. "I sat in my car waiting for Justin when Evan came to the car and started pounding on it." She shivered, but not from cold.

"Did he threaten you?"

"He pounded on my window and told me to get out. He got angry when I wouldn't. He told me I'd be sorry." Evan's glaring eyes and tight face swam in her head. *You're gonna be fuckin' sorry!* She could hear the hatred in his voice.

"Is there a restraining order in place?"

"Not yet, officer," said Justin. "But after today there will be one."

The officer nodded and walked over to his partner. They talked for a few minutes out of everyone's hearing. Angela moved close and laced her arm around Emily, watching the police talk. Emily leaned against her, grateful for her little sister's presence.

Evan paced the road across from them, shooting angry stares at Emily. She half expected him to sprint across the street with his arms outstretched, ready to strangle her.

The officers broke away and approached the curious neighbors. They asked a few questions, then moved on to a few other houses. They didn't take long however, but met up again, and talked one last time.

The officer returned. "We're going to arrest Mr. Waters for Breach of Peace and that should take care of things for tonight. But if you are going to get a restraining order, do it first thing in the morning. Don't wait."

The other officer handcuffed Evan and put him in the police car.

Evan shot one last glance at Emily, one filled with anger and hate. "Are you fucking him too, Emily?" shouted Evan, nodding his head toward Justin.

The police officer took her former boyfriend's arm and guided him firmly into the police car as Emily burst into tears. She wished the ground below her would open and then swallow her up. Anything was better than this. Anything.

Chapter Six

Consequences

Reger rubbed against Emily's legs as she tried to serve coffee to Justin and Angela.

"Poor Reger," Emily cooed. She had managed to compose herself again after the police cruiser had left with Evan in the back seat. She set the cups down on the counter and picked up her orange tabby.

Justin sat on the stool at the counter facing the kitchen.

Angela, standing behind Emily, leaned toward the kitchen window peering out onto the street. "The car's still here. Which means he'll be back for it."

"The officer said I should be okay for tonight." She rubbed her face against Reger's soft fur, hiding her fear so Angela wouldn't see it. She glanced over at Justin.

Justin shook his head before taking a sip of his coffee. "Breach of Peace is a misdemeanor. He can bond out at the police station. He could be back here tonight."

"Emily!" Angela quickly stepped back from the window, as if a brick might come through it... "I think you should stay with me tonight."

"I have work in the morning, and—"

"Emily," said Justin firmly. "Angela's right. You can't be here alone. It's not safe."

"I can't keep hiding because of one idiot."

"You're right." Justin sighed. "It's not fair. But it's more important that you're safe. If you don't want to stay with Angela, stay with your parents, but until we have that restraining order, you shouldn't be alone in this apartment. Does he still have a key to it?"

Emily rubbed the back of her neck. She didn't want to agree, but Justin made sense. Already Evan disrupted her work and her love life. "I don't know about the key. He could still have his or have made a new one. I'm not sure." She sighed. "Okay, Justin. But just for tonight. I can't keep leaving my cat alone because Evan's an asshole."

Angela snorted. "Emily!" she chided softly.

"What? He is, isn't he?"

"Yes." Angela nodded and then shook her head. "But what would Father Peters say if he heard you?"

Justin drank the last of his coffee and set it down. "He'd say," said Justin, "that Evan was being an asshole, though probably he'd have a biblical phrase for it. Like a crevice or something." He looked back and forth at the two of them. "Not funny?"

Angela shook her head.

Emily giggled despite Angela's motherly look of disdain.

Justin winked at her, his head tilted perfectly so Angela would see it. "Pack a small bag, Emily. I've got to get Angela home."

"You go. I have to speak to Mrs. Diggerty and get my things together. I'll be there shortly."

"You sure?" Angela set her glass in the sink.

"Yes. He's not going to show up in the next ten minutes! It'll take him a while to finish things at the police station, won't it?"

"Yes," said Justin. "A couple of hours at least."

"Good. It's settled. Go along and I'll be there in an hour. Don't worry. I'll be fine."

When they finally left she hurried to fill an overnight back and feed Reger a little more cat food. "Be good, Reger. Mind the house while I'm gone." She hurried over to Mrs. Diggerty's door and knocked hard so the older woman would hear her. "Mrs. Diggerty!"

"Oh, Emily," she said, opening the door. "How are you?"

"Did you see the police?" She felt terrible going straight to that but otherwise she'd be standing for an hour talking about the weather or a recipe before they got to the real reason she had come to talk to Mrs. Diggerty.

"Yes. What were they here for?"

"Evan's been bothering me. I'm going to spend the night at my sister's house, and I won't be back probably until tomorrow after work. Can you watch Reger for me?"

"Of course, dear."

"If you see Evan in the building, call the police. He shouldn't be here. Tomorrow, I'm getting a restraining order to keep him away."

"Oh, that serious? I'm sorry, dear. Yes. I'll take care of Reger. Don't worry. You take care of you."

Emily wondered a moment if Mrs. Diggerty would be safe as well. Evan was an asshole, but not an idiot. She knew he wouldn't bother her. She gave Mrs. Diggerty a kiss on the cheek. "You've been wonderful. Thank you very much."

"You be careful, Emily."

"I will. You too. I'll see you tomorrow. I'll get back as soon as I finish work. Minus traffic commute."

"No rush. I'll enjoy the company of your tabby. Be careful," she reminded Emily again.

Emily nodded, close to tears. She made her escape and came out on the porch, looking around carefully, watching to see if Evan might be lurking anywhere. A light breeze rustled the new leaves on the oak trees that lined the street and she started at the sudden sound. Emily felt ridiculous, but on the other hand, Evan showed up unexpectedly twice today. When she walked past her car, the vehicle she put so much money in, a thread of sadness wound around her heart. In a way, the car reminded her of Luke, something she could have for a moment, but never possess on her own.

When she got inside her sister's car, her nerves steadied, but only because she felt safer than walking in the open. She put on her headset and put her phone on the seat beside her. Her overprotective little sister would be calling her to check on her progress in getting to her apartment. She checked her phone one more time on the off chance that Luke called her, then kicked herself for being disappointed when he didn't. He showed his true colors by taking up with Sheila Harmon at the first opportunity. All the talk of getting married? Yeah. That was just a line of patter to keep her interested in putting out. When she cooled on him, he was on to the next conquest.

The sadness tied tighter around her heart as she passed Walkerville's city limits into Westfield. Instead of taking the highway, she'd taken the secondary road that ran parallel to it, thinking to stop at a Walgreens to pick up a few things. She needed toothpaste for one thing, and other personal items just in case. Emily pulled into the first pharmacy she saw.

It didn't occur to her until she saw Luke's SUV in the parking lot that she was in his neighborhood. She sat in her car staring at it and then decided she was being silly. They lived within ten miles of each other. They were bound to bump into each other from time to time. Ironic that they hadn't for the past ten years prior.

What was she supposed to do? Avoid every man she ever had a relationship with?

Still, it took more courage than she thought she possessed to get out of the car and walk into the pharmacy. She just needed a few things, and it was a large store. There was no need to see him at all, especially if she moved quickly – at least that was the lame excuse she told herself.

She grabbed a basket and began tossing the stuff she needed as fast as she could. It was one thing to be brave outside the store, an entirely other thing to be inside so close to him seeing her before she spotted him. She kept her head down as she shopped, hoping he might have already left and not even noticed her sister's car parked outside.

She stopped short when she came to the end of the aisle and saw Luke standing on crutches in line at the pharmacy. The nervous butterflies in her stomach felt like a swarm of bees as she watched him. He was in his own world, oblivious that she was even there.

He stared straight ahead, slightly swaying on the crutches. She couldn't get a good look at his face, but his whole body seemed drawn tense as if he were in pain. She felt her eyes widen when she saw the patch of red blood at the back of his jeans. She debated walking over to him and saying something to him, but then he moved to speak to the pharmacist and the moment was gone. Instead, she hurried to a cash register at the front of the store and quickly paid for her items.

Emily slipped into the car, but couldn't find it in herself to turn over the engine. She sat staring at Luke's SUV, longing to talk to him but not having the courage to. Her sister said he had been with Sheila. That's probably how he got the knife wound – two women were fighting over him. She shook her head at the crazy thought.

Finally, he hobbled out of the store and climbed in, his face drawn in tight lines. It killed her to see him looking like he did. Jealousy aside, she didn't like him hurting. She longed to say or do something, anything to ease the pain etched around those beautiful eyes.

Emily shook her head as she started her car. She was just getting herself into a mess thinking about him.

She didn't have any excuse as to why she ended up behind him, though she hung back. His SUV swayed back and forth slightly, and she bit her lip. It was clear he shouldn't be driving.

"It's none of your business, Emily Rose Dougherty," she told herself sternly. But instead of turning off on the road that would take her to her sister's apartment, she followed Luke. "Just to make sure he makes it home okay," she murmured to herself.

As she drove, the anxiety of the day piled onto her thoughts of Luke. She decided he deserved a piece of her mind. He had no business treating her like he did, fucking her, and then moving on. He was a jerk, an ass, and any other nasty name she could think of. He was nearly as bad as Evan. Nearly.

When Luke turned into his parking lot, she chickened out. She drove past the entrance and found herself on Main Street, Westfield, the streets clogged with evening traffic. Emily grew annoyingly frustrated by the way-too-many one-way streets. It took her an interminable length of time to find the right combination that brought her to the right direction back to her sister's house. Even when she did, the traffic was so slow she was barely moving at ten miles per hour.

Her phone chimed.

"Damn," she swore and clicked the phone on through her headset. As she predicted earlier, it was Angela.

"Emily, are you okay?" Angela, as usual, worried too much about Emily.

"Yes. I just missed the turnoff to your road and have been trying to navigate the damned one-way streets of Westfield."

Angela laughed. "I never go downtown if I don't have to. How'd you end up there?"

"I missed your street and also stopped at Walgreens to grab a toothbrush and some other stuff."

"Gotchya."

"I believe I'm finally travelling in the right direction. It'll take me a bit, I think the entire town is out in their cars right now."

Angela chuckled. "Take your time. No reckless driving."

"Ha. Funny, sister. Very funny." Emily smiled despite herself. "I should be there in about fifteen-twenty minutes, barring any road rage I may suffer."

"Glad your humor's still intact." Angela laughed again. "See you soon."

Emily clicked off the phone and stared out the front window and sighed. It had been a horrible day. She wanted to think she was a victim, but she knew she was also responsible for letting things happen. She banged her fist against the steering wheel. She was tired of other people dictating the terms of her life. Emily was sick of people doing what they wanted to her without thought or care of how it affected her. Furious that she'd allowed other people to do things that messed up her life. Evan was an ass. Everybody could see that and if they couldn't, they were idiots.

As she inched toward Luke's apartment complex, she glared in his direction. Luke was a dick. How dare he get involved with criminals, tainting her chance to be with him!

A driver cut in front of her suddenly, forcing her to hit her brakes.

"Fuck you!" she yelled. Then she realized she wanted to say those very words to Luke Wade.

"Siri," she said to her iPhone roughly, "Call Luke."

The phone rang but went to voice mail, "This is Luke. You know what to do."

Emily hit her hands against the steering wheel again. Fire burned inside of her. No! He wasn't going to get away with not answering his phone. She knew she was close to the entrance of his complex's parking lot. There was a small space in the line of cars and impulsively she cut sharply across it, sparking a round of angry honks of horns by other drivers. She didn't care. She flipped the bird to anyone who might be glaring at her.

She parked and slammed the car door shut, her heart beating wildly. Never before had she done anything resembling this. Emily had always been the good girl, always compliant, doing what she was told. She decided she had enough of that, and for the first time in her life, she wasn't going to let herself be walked over.

The first thing on her list was telling Luke Wade exactly what she thought about him.

Her feet thundered up the stairs to the second floor while her heart matched her angry footfalls beat by beat. When she reached his door she didn't use the doorbell. She struck the door hard with her fist several times, her jaw clenched tight.

The door flew open. Instead of Luke, a woman stood in the doorframe, a slice of pizza in her hand and a freakin' happy smile on her face.

Emily's eyes narrowed. It'd been ten years, but she'd recognize Sheila Harmon anywhere. Her long dark hair and brown eyes hadn't changed a bit. "I'm here to see Luke."

"He's laying down." Sheila's big brown eyes ran down and then up Emily, as if trying to remember who she was.

Emily shoved her way in. "Good. Then he won't fall so hard when I kick his ass."

"Hey!" protested Sheila, following her.

But Emily didn't listen. She marched in Luke's bedroom and glared at him stretched out on his bed.

"Em?" he said with a lazy smile. He was obviously in no pain now.

"What the fuck, Luke! What's wrong with you?" She sucked in a sharp breath. "I tell you we need to cool things for a while and what do you do?" She shook her head, disgusted. "The first chance you get, you take up with Sheila Harmon! *Sheila Harmon?* Your old high school flame." She put so much venom in these last words she surprised herself. "You working on your own personal high school reunion?"

Luke struggled to sit up. "It's not like that, Em. At all. She's a nurse. She was helping me."

She glared at him, he sounded hammered. "Oh! So you were playing doctor?"

Luke righted himself and swung his legs to the floor. "Don't be ridiculous," he snapped.

His anger set hers over the edge. "Ridiculous? I'm being ridiculous? Then what is she doing here now?"

"I told you."

"With pizza and laughter? That some kind of medicine therapy? Maybe a blowjob for dessert? Well, fuck you, Luke Wade!" Emily turned and fled out of the bedroom to his living room. Sheila was gone and the front door hung open. She couldn't believe what she had just said to him. Face burning, she sped across the floor but a strong arm jerked her back, whipping her around to come face to face with Luke.

He stood there with an incredibly pissed-off look, barely able to hold himself up on the single crutch he'd grabbed in his haste to stop her. His eyes blazed as they glared at each other, both their chests heaving. "Do I get at least the courtesy of an explanation about what the hell's going on before you run away again?" He waited for her to respond and when she didn't, he pressed her again. "Well? Do I, Emily?"

Chapter Seven

Truth

Emily's breath caught. It felt like she was standing in a ring of fire from the glare coming from Luke's face. His hand gripped her arm tightly. Too tightly. It began to hurt something fierce.

"Well, Emily?" he said, his face grim. "You running again?"

She lifted her chin. "Let go of my arm! You're hurting me."

Luke instantly loosened his hold, but he continued to stare at her as if trying to will her to speak.

She swallowed hard. Standing this close to him suddenly jumbled her thoughts. He looked so gorgeous and smelled way too damn good. Except she was angry at him too. It wasn't about Sheila Harmon, though that did tick her off. She was angry because Luke had made her life impossible by dangling his sexy self in front of her, and yet he was too dangerous to hold. She wanted him, but if she took him, her life would spin much more out of control than it already had. "I just can't do this again," she said in a trembling voice. "I have too much to lose."

"Do you, Emily?" Luke said bitterly. "What would you lose? A family that can't let you grow up? A boyfriend that's intent on screwing you over?"

She blinked. He didn't understand. "My job. My life."

"How about love, Emily? Are you willing to lose that for any of those other things?"

"What kind of love, Luke? A love where I can't be sure where you are, what you're doing and who you're doing it with?"

"Nothing happened with Sheila."

"Maybe something did, maybe it didn't." She sighed and threw her hands up in the air. "This isn't about Sheila Harmon.

In the one day we're apart, you end up in a bar fight, apparently a bad knife wound, and have another woman in your apartment." She shook her head. "Don't try to defend yourself. Normal men don't do that, Luke."

"I never said I was normal." He leaned his weight on the single crutch.

"And that's just it, isn't it? Even when you were in high school you just had to push boundaries, had to be a rebel."

"You liked that."

"No! I never liked that! I liked you. I loved you. I loved the boy under the leather and the attitude. I loved your sweetheart, how you always looked after me, how you cared enough about me not to push me farther than I was willing to go."

Luke made a face like he didn't believe her. "If you loved all that, why did you abandon me? Why didn't you visit me while I was stuck in a hospital bed all fucking summer?"

"Because I had to choose!" She knew he wouldn't understand how much it had hurt her as well. "I had to decide between my future and a boy who was heading into serious trouble. Everyone told me that, and I wasn't blind to it. I could have chosen you, Luke, and lost everything else I wanted. I could have stayed and ended up with no education and a bunch of kids who would have lost their father because he did something stupid. You weren't ready, and neither was I, for the kind of commitment you wanted."

Luke's hand dropped from her arm and Emily thought that he'd given up. She hated that thought and wanted to take back everything she just said. How could she be so callous?

"You're right," he said, swaying on his feet. "I did get into trouble. It was bad. I thought I got into trouble because after you left I had nothing to live for. But, looking at it now, I'd have done it whether you were there or not. I don' blame y'Emily." His last words were slurred and as he lurched toward his bedroom he stumbled.

"Luke!" Emily rushed to keep him from falling. She pulled back on his arm and he straightened. She wedged herself under his shoulder to hold him up. "Come on. I'll help you back to bed."

"Damn painkillers," he mumbled. "Did'n know they were this strong."

"Lean on me," she said, hating to see him in pain again. He was always incredibly strong and when he showed weakness, it scared her. "I'll hold you up."

"You always do."

She helped him to his bed and steadied him as he sat on the edge. "Lay down," she commanded.

"The room's spinning," he groaned and buried his face in his hands. "Get me the wastebasket." He gulped. "Please."

Emily glanced around the bedroom. She found it and handed it to him just in time for him to lose his pizza.

Chapter Eight

And Consequences

Luke's gut wrenched as he vomited. Cold, then heat burned through him.

"Lay down." Emily reached for the wastebasket and set it down. "I won't be able to pick you up if you fall on the floor."

She lifted his legs and he turned and curled up on the bed. Everything felt very far away except for the cramps that hit his stomach. He curled into the fetal position, wishing he could just pass out and then wake up feeling normal.

Eyes shut tight, Luke heard some papers rustling and then Emily on the phone.

"Yes. I'm calling about Luke Wade. He was released from the emergency room this morning after a knife wound? Yeah. He just vomited and looks very pale. He's been complaining that he's dizzy... Yes, I'll wait."

The room spun some more. Time seemed to stop and then started when Emily spoke again, "I'll check."

Luke felt Emily's hand on his forehead.

"No, he doesn't seem to have a fever. I'm not exactly sure." She paused while someone spoke into the phone. Luke felt her lips close to his ear. "Luke, they're asking how many Percocet you took."

"One," he groaned. "Just before I ate."

"He took one less than an hour ago." More silence.

"Okay. I'll make sure he isn't alone, and I'll call if a fever develops. Thanks."

There were a few seconds of quiet and for Luke it seemed like he was disconnected from the world.

"Hey, Ang. I think it's better if I check into a hotel. I've been thinking... Evan knows where you live and might look for me there. I know, I know... It's just better if I'm not where he can find me... No. I'll be okay. I'll just watch a movie and get some sleep. I'm exhausted... Yes, I'll call you if there are any problems. Can you tell Justin to meet me at the diner for breakfast? Then we'll talk about getting that restraining order in place. About seven, okay? What? Oh. I'll call my boss now. Yeah, I'm not happy about that, but I got legal eagle Justin on my side. It'll work out... Love you, too."

Silence.

"Mr. Hobson. I'm sorry I have to leave this message on your answering machine, but I can't come in tomorrow morning. I know you won't be happy but, unfortunately, it can't be avoided. I should've told you what happened this morning to make me late. That's what my lawyer told me. I'll explain it to you tomorrow afternoon as soon as I can. I'm truly sorry. Thank you for your understanding."

Luke felt the other side of his bed sink a moment later.

"The good news is that you're probably having a reaction to the Percocet, and it'll work itself out of your system. The nurse I spoke to said you should try to sleep. I'll stay and keep an eye on you."

Luke fought the grogginess. "Em, are you in some kind of double? I mean danger." He shook his head trying to clear it. "I mean trouble."

She slid next to him and put her arms around his neck. "Oh yeah," she said softly and then kissed his forehead.

"You don't need to stay," he protested weakly.

"Buddy, you can't make me leave."

Luke woke in the dark finding Emily's arm around his waist. He was confused at first, but as his head cleared, so did his memory. Emily was angry with him, and yet she'd stayed when it looked like he was in trouble. He pressed against her, taking in her sweet scent.

Even though his thigh hurt, he felt better than earlier in the evening. The dizziness and nausea were gone. He grinned. And Emily was in his arms.

She stirred against him. He felt her heart fluttering against his chest. "Luke? Is everything okay?" she murmured sleepily.

"Yes. Thanks, Em, for watching out for me."

"You don't have to thank me," she said softly.

"It feels right having you here."

Emily stiffened in his arms. "I don't think Father Peters would think so."

"Father Peters?" The name sounded familiar and then Luke remembered the priest who talked with him. "Is he your priest?"

"Yes," Emily whispered.

"I see," he said, not wanting to anger the priest who had spoken kindly and without judgement to him. "Then maybe you should go home."

"What? No. I mean."

Luke pulled her tighter. "Some time, some day, Emily, you're going to have to decide whether you'll live your life or have other people do it for you."

Emily sighed, a long, sad sounding thing in the darkness. "It's just so hard being taught one thing all of my life and finding out..." Her voice faded.

"What, Emily, what did you find out?"

"That everything I believed doesn't fit with what I want."

"Welcome to the real world, sweetheart." Luke kissed the top of her head. "It doesn't have to go against what you believe. You just might have to open your heart or your mind to a different way to look at it."

"Every time I try to do the right thing, it turns out bad. All my life I was taught that all I had to do was the right thing, obey my parents, get good grades in school, go out with the 'right' boys. But it doesn't work. I'm still in trouble, my ex-boyfriend, the one my parents love so much, is a dick, and the one man..."

"What, Em?" Luke asked gently.

"The one man I love is someone no one wants me to have." She whispered these words.

"You know what, Emily?"

"What?"

"You think too much." With that he crushed his mouth on her soft lips. Her sweetness sent fire through him. His only thought was that he wanted more of her and he pushed in his tongue to claim her mouth. He cupped her ass with his hand and pulled her into him. He was hard and the sensation of her hips against his drove him to a fever pitch. Luke couldn't stop tasting or touching her. Unlike times with other lovers, there was no thought for technique or the right moves. Emily trembled in his arms, her own kisses growing more frantic, as if she wanted to melt into him.

Luke pushed up her dress and unclasped her bra, freeing her breasts. He pulled the dress and the bra over her head, loving the feel of her soft skin against his chest. Luke pushed his face into her breasts and kissed and licked until he found her nipples. He sucked one in and swirled the nub with the tip of his tongue. Emily moaned and when he drew the tip of her breast deeper in his mouth, she hissed and arched her back.

He couldn't help but to press his erection into her cleft, the only thing holding them back was the fabric of their underwear between them.

It didn't take long before that wasn't enough. Having enough, he pulled down her panties, and pushed down his own boxers. She shivered when he pressed into her again, this time bare skin against skin. He pressed his shaft against her clit. She palmed the tip of it, smearing his precum over the head.

He couldn't take it. Luke needed to be in her now.

Dimly, he remembered the condoms in the nightstand, and he clumsily pulled one out. His hand trembled as he opened the package and rolled it on. He settled in between her legs, and zeroed in on the other tit, sweeping the nub with his tongue and biting it lightly.

Emily's breathing hitched when his teeth met her flesh. His hand reached between her thighs and found heaven as her juices melted over his fingers.

"I'm taking you now, Emily. No more discussion. No more uncertainty. You're mine."

He lined his cock to her center and thrust into her tight core. She gasped but wrapped her legs around his waist taking him deeper. His cock pulsed in response to her heat and tightness. Luke pulled back and thrust in harder and she pushed her hips to meet him. His cock became fiercer and seeking more of her. The harder he pushed the more she groaned. Years of wanting her poured through him into her and she took it all, demanding more. And he gave it, seeking to sear her soul with his want and need of her so she always understood that it was only her that claimed him.

"Luke!" she screamed as she clenched around him, bucking her hips. His name ringing in his ears he exploded, driving as deep into her as he possibly could.

They held on to each other tightly as their breathing slowed. She melted into his arms and settled against his chest.

"Mine," he gasped. "You're not getting away from me again."

Chapter Nine

Busy Morning

Emily shook her head as she looked at Luke's wound. "It started bleeding again," she said as she peeled back the slightly red-soaked bandage.

Luke smiled lazily at her. "What? From a wee little bit of activity?"

Emily's face drew into a frown but she couldn't hold it and started chuckling. "I'd hardly call it wee little."

"Just give me a few days, and I'll be able to give you a better sense of proportion." He turned his head and winked at her.

"Uh huh. Now lay still so I can change your bandage." She crawled over him across the bed to collect the first aid things on the dresser. She grabbed a bowl of water and began cleaning around the wound.

"Hey!" cried Luke as some soap accidentally hit the open cut.

"You, mister, need to keep your leg up during the day and give that thing a chance to close. You need to heal." She applied another large gauze bandage and taped the edges.

"Yes, ma'am." He smirked. "I'll be a good boy. Until you get home, that is."

"We'll see," she said more soberly, not wanting to think about the day. She patted the side of his thigh and checked the clock radio on the nightstand. "Okay, you're set. I have to go and meet my lawyer. I'll bring you back some breakfast. What do you like?"

Luke reached up and pulled her down to his chest. "You. I'd like you over-easy with a side of delicious."

"That may be all you'll get." She tried to sound like she was scolding him, but his words made her insides tingle.

"Mmm," he said, smacking his lips.

"Incorrigible." She smiled and kissed his mouth. "Now you have to let me up. I don't want to be late. Some people have to get to work."

"I thought you called in to say you couldn't be there."

"I'm talking to my lawyer. Now, while I'm away, don't let in any strange women." She walked out of the bedroom.

"Yes, ma'am," he called out.

She poked her head in the bedroom doorway and winked. "Especially ones you know."

"Get out of here." He threw a pillow at her and laughed. "I'll be here when you get back, with nothing on but the radio."

She grinned wickedly at him. "I'll count on it."

Luke lay his head back on the pillow. Now that they knew he reacted badly to the Percocet he had her flush the pills down the toilet. Luke found when Emily was near he didn't need the painkillers anyway. Just her touch soothed him. Of course, now that she was gone his leg throbbed some, but if he kept still it didn't bother him too much. No, the pain and burn came when he got up to go to the bathroom or shuffle to the kitchen, even with the crutches for help.

When Emily left he could admit to himself he felt tired, especially after this early morning's activities. He was just drifting off to sleep when his phone rang.

He grabbed it off the nightstand. "Yeah," he said.

"Saks, boss. You want me to open up?"

"Yeah, that would be great. I'm supposed to stay off my leg a couple days. Think you can hold the fort?"

"What about Gibs? Two men can't run a four-man shop."

"I'll call him. There's no reason I know of why he shouldn't be at work."

"What about payroll?" Saks coughed.

Oh damn. He forgot about payroll. Some of the guys lived paycheck to paycheck. "Can you bring the time cards and the checkbook tonight? I'll do it here."

"You sure, boss?"

"Just keep making the deposits. Did you remember to process the credit cards last night?"

"Uh... no. I don't know how to do it."

"Hmph. I thought I showed you. Well, tell Gibs when he arrives. He knows how."

"Okay, boss. Anything else?"

"Yeah. Get to work."

"Sure, boss." The line went dead.

Luke gave a little shake of his head and called Gibs.

"Hey, Luke," said Helen. "How're you feeling?"

"Managing all right. Is Gibs in?"

"Just a sec... Frank! Luke's on the phone for you."

Luke waited while Gibs picked up the phone.

"Hey. Luke. What's up?"

"Just checking up on you."

"I'm fine." Gibs' voice dropped to a whisper. "I'll have the money for you today."

"I'm not worried about that. I just want to make sure you get your ass to work."

"Yeah, sure," Gibs said in a more normal voice. "Helen wants to know if you need anything."

"No, I'm good. I just need to keep off this leg a bit. Oh, and Saks didn't process the credit cards last night, so you need to."

"Okay, I'll see if I remember how to do that."

"Call customer service if you have a problem. The number is on the credit card machine. They'll walk you through it."

"Sure, Luke. Hey, I just want to thank you for everything."

"Well, I expect an explanation, but that can wait until later."

"Okay, Luke. Gotta go. The boss expects me to get into work."

"That's a tough boss you have there," said Luke.

"Yeah. He's a dickhead but I still like him." Gibs chuckled. "I'll stop by."

Before Luke could tell him not to bother, Gibs ended the call.

He lay back his head expecting to get a nap. A knock on the door told him that wasn't going to happen. He hobbled on his crutches to the door, wondering who was there. When he pulled it open he was surprised to see two men who had the whiff of 'cop' wafting from them.

"Yes?" said Luke. "Can I help you?"

"I'm Detective Price and this is Detective Anglotti. Can we come in?"

Luke glared at the detectives. His experience with the police taught him not to trust any of them. "Um, no. This isn't a good time for me. I'm supposed to be resting."

"Yes," said Price, staring at Luke's crutches. "From a knife wound. Care to tell us what happened?"

"I gave my statement at the Emergency Room to your boys, Ignati and Ricci."

"Well, it wasn't a statement you signed, Mr. Wade. And we need a statement for our file."

"I'll tell you what. When I'm recovered I'll come down to the station." Luke started to shut the door but Price put his hand on it.

"I understand one of your employees was arrested for drug trafficking."

"Yes."

"And you bailed him out."

"True. What's the point here?" Luke tried to keep his voice neutral but his irritation managed to sneak through.

"You and Mr. Gibson belong to the Hades' Spawn Motorcycle Club."

"Apparently you know everything about me."

"Do we, Mr. Wade? I wonder. Wasn't your club president arrested on those some charges?"

"Again, correct. If I had any lollipops I'd give you one as a reward."

"Mr. Wade, we aren't joking here. Two out of twenty members of your club have been arrested for drug sales in the past months. That's more than what we call a coincidence."

"Excuse me for being cranky. I'm in more than a little pain."

"Is it possible that your little mix-up the other night was connected with other things?"

"Sure. It was connected with some asshole playing mumbly-pegs in the bar and losing control of his blade."

"Really, that's not what you told our officers."

"Really? Because I didn't tell them shit, because there wasn't anything to tell. It was an accident and there is no sense getting into some stupid fuck's face for getting clumsy."

"So that's your story. Your *new* story."

"Do you have a point to make?"

"We'd rather you'd cooperate with us."

"I'm sure. I'm just not sure what I'm supposed to cooperate with. Assumptions and innuendoes? That doesn't seem to make good police work, fellas. Now, if you'll excuse me, I'm under doctor's orders to rest this leg. Good day."

"Mr. Wade," said Price in a warning tone. But Luke shut the door, putting it between him and the two cops. What was happening? Why were the police insinuating he had something to do with drug running?

His phone vibrated in his pocket. Luke didn't recognize the number but answered it anyway. "This is Luke," he snapped.

An automated voice spit out an announcement of how this was a pre-paid call from Enfield Correctional Institution from Oklahoma Walker and to press "one" if he wanted to take the call. Cops at the door and now Okie's calling from jail? If they were eavesdropping outside, this would really get their heads spinning. Luke pressed 'one'. "Okie?" he said. "How are you?"

"As good as you can expect," he said in his gravelly voice. Okie was twenty years older than Luke but looked and sounded like forty years more. "How are 'ya doing?"

"Same old."

"Don't give me that shit, Spade. It doesn't take long for shit to travel from the streets to here. I hear a certain friend of an old friend got you good."

"Don't believe everything you hear, Okie. Some guys just don't know how to be a good sport about things. He's banned from the Red Bull if that gives you a clue."

Okie started laughing, a strangled sound, like he hadn't laughed in a while.

"Good. I know I told all you guys to stay away, and I still want that. But I'm sending you some birthday wishes anyway."

Luke frowned. His birthday passed weeks ago. But Okie was trying to tell him something, perhaps something he couldn't say over the phone.

"Well, thanks, man. It ain't the same without you here."

"Yeah. I miss all you guys too. Well, most of you guys. Gotta go. Be careful, son. Take care of yourself."

"Is there anything you need?"

"Just my goddamn club in one piece for when I'm outta here," growled Okie, then he hung up the phone.

By now Luke's leg was throbbing. He decided he needed to get off the leg and think over things. Okie was upset about something. A call like Luke just got should have gone to the Prez, VP or the Treasurer of the club. That Okie called Luke signaled something was seriously wrong with the leadership. And that wasn't a good thought.

Just when he was about to hobble back to his bed there was another knock on the door.

"What now!" sputtered Luke. He yanked the door open. Gibs stood there, his eyes wide. "What the hell, Gibs. Why aren't you at work?"

"I just wanted to give you this. Sorry if I disturbed you." Gibs thrust an envelope at Luke's chest. He had no choice but to grab it.

"What's this?"

"The five grand. I pulled it out of savings."

"I told you not to worry about it."

"And I appreciate that. But you didn't deserve to get dragged into this and I'm sure as hell not going to keep you on the hook for money I should have paid. And as far as your bikes, man, I'll show up at court. Don't you worry."

"Oh, I'm not worried. I'll drag you in there myself."

"Okay. I'll get into work now."

"I'd appreciate it. Saks is pulling his hair out."

"Yeah," grinned Gibs. "Sharp dressing doesn't mean sharp thinking."

"Out!"

"Bye."

Luke shut the door one more time and started for his bedroom once again when his doorbell rang.

"What the fuck!" exploded Luke as he pulled the door so hard the handle flew out of his hand.

Helen, Gibs' wife gasped. "Sorry, Luke. It seems I caught you at a bad time."

"You and everyone else."

The small woman swallowed hard. "I was wondering if I could talk to you."

Luke half nodded, half shook his head. He was sure this was a conversation he didn't want to have.

"Come in, Helen. Have a seat."

Helen crossed into his apartment and sat on a chair kitty-corner to his sofa. He sat carefully on the couch, putting his leg up.

"So, what's up, Helen?"

"You can start by telling me the truth about what happened a couple nights ago."

Luke shrugged. "A guy at the Red Bull was playing mumbly pegs and lost control of his knife. It landed in the back of my leg."

"Bullshit," she said vehemently.

Luke sat back in the couch and stared at Helen, whose face was turning a shade of red.

"Sorry, Luke. But I'm so tired of all the lies. I know he spends time running with the guys in the club, and I'm okay with that. Hell, with a man like Frank either you are okay with it, or you pack up and go home to momma. But Frank has been acting strange lately. He's quiet and all into himself. He barely speaks to me. Now he disappeared for more than a day and he isn't talking about where he had been. Luke, I'm begging you. Please tell me what's going on."

Luke shook his head. "I don't get in the middle of married people's business, Helen. I'm sorry. You'll just have to get him to tell you."

Helen looked away. A tear dripped down her cheek and she brushed it away. "But it isn't good, is it, Luke?"

Luke's mouth ran dry so he shook his head. "Sorry, Helen."

Chapter Eleven

Questions

Emily sat in the Walkerville Diner sipping on her coffee, waiting for Justin. A copy of the *New Haven Journal* lay out on the counter and she pulled it to her. On the local page a story caught her eye.

Dust Up at Local Watering Hole Leaves Police Baffled

An incident at the Red Bull Bar and Grille last Monday leaves local law enforcement without answers. At approximately 11:30 PM Police were called to the scene of an incident involving local business owner Luke Wade and an unknown assailant. Mr. Wade suffered an injury that required transport to Middletown Hospital for treatment. However, no witnesses have been found or have come forward to report the incident.

Employees of the Red Bull report they did not see the altercation, which happened in the parking lot of the establishment.

The Red Bull caters to the biker crowd, though for most of its thirty-year history, have not had any incidents, which required police involvement.

The owner of the bar, Shelton Rocco says, "We are deeply grieved that Mr. Wade, a longtime customer, and friend, suffered an injury while at the Red Bull. We at the Red Bull do everything we can to foster an environment where those who love the freedom of the open road can relax with like-minded people."

The Westfield Police Department urges anyone with information to call either Detective Price or Detective Anglotti at 860-555-7072.

Emily swallowed. What did Luke get into? Or why would someone try and hurt him? Tough on the outside, she had the feeling he was still soft on the inside like he was in high school. She kicked herself for not questioning him why he had that injury. More to the point, was he in danger? She had Evan to be concerned with and here she was, more worried about Luke than herself.

Justin slid onto the stool beside her. "You sleep all right? How was the hotel?"

He seemed to be questioning why she went to a hotel without directly asking. She stared down at her coffee, hoping she didn't smell like she'd gone to Luke's instead. "I thought it would be best. Evan knows where Angela lives and I didn't want to chance him showing up there and bothering her."

"Well, she didn't hear anything from him, but she's worried about you." Direct this time.

"I'm fine. Really, Justin." She turned to meet his gaze. "I just needed some alone time. Angela worrying over me is not helping my stress level."

Justin stared at her and then grinned. "She is a little overprotective, of everyone. You should see her during flu season. She has me using that disinfecting gel everywhere I go."

Emily smiled. "Yep, that's Angela. She made me use it when I was a kid, too."

Justin pointed to a booth and picked up his briefcase. "You ready to get this done?"

"Yes." She followed him to the empty booth, carrying her coffee mug. "What do I have to do?"

"I've filled out this form asking for a protective order." He pulled it out from his briefcase. "It's a request for a temporary order. You'll have to go to court in a week or so for the hearing to get a permanent request."

"Does that mean I'll have to see him?"

"You'll be in the same courtroom, yes, but I'll be with you. But for now, what you need to do is go to the Superior Courthouse, to the clerk's office on the second floor."

"You're not going with me?"

"No. You don't need me there. It would just be a waste of your retainer money and I have another case I have to prep for. This is the one filing where you don't have to pay any fees, so don't worry about that. Hand the papers to the clerk and he or she will take it from there. Wait until they come back with a signed order from the judge. Let them know that Evan's in court today and that'll make it easier for the marshal to serve him the papers. They'll serve him right in the courthouse. This'll take a while so expect to spend a few hours there." He glanced up at her. "You'll be fine. Once the papers are served to Evan, he'll know. If he shows up anywhere near you, call the police."

Emily nodded. "Thanks, Justin." She didn't see how a restraining order was going to stop him. If he showed up, she had to call the police? That wasn't going to stop him from trying to get in her apartment, or car, or workplace until a cruiser showed up. At least it was something. Better than nothing.

"Now sign these forms, here, and here, and I'll sign them. That's all the paperwork done. The court doors open in, let's see..." He looked at his iPhone. "An hour and a half. The sooner you get there the easier it'll be for the marshal to get him served before he leaves the courthouse." His phone began buzzing and he swiped through his messages. "I have to get to the office now. Call me if you need anything."

"Thanks, Justin."

"No problem. Give your sister a call. She's worried about you."

"Okay, I'll do that."

He nodded and hurried out of the diner.

Emily ordered three fried egg and bacon sandwiches to go; one for her, the other two for Luke. The extra one was a hedge against a man's hunger. Emily didn't know how much Luke ate, though judging what little was left of the pizza Monday night he could pack it away when it suited him.

She paid for the food with her debit card after she checked the balance on her banking app on her phone. Emily winced when she saw the bank balance of her savings, which displayed on the same screen as her checking account. Paying the bond for her release and Justin's retainer knocked the balance down significantly.

The reason she didn't want to buy a car outright with her savings was that she didn't want to lose that bank balance which was a nice barrier against disaster. Now her strategy backfired on her and she was paying more than if she paid for the car herself. And she didn't even have the car now. She hated that it made her feel stupid. She shouldn't have given so much power to one man. She was so obsessed about placing distance between her parents that she made a decision that banked on a man's trustworthiness to work. Ultimately, Evan was not only untrustworthy, but he was also dangerously possessive as well. How had she gotten herself into this mess without realizing? Man, she needed to change her life around. Which brought her back to Luke.

What about him? He got into some sort of knife fight that left him with a nasty cut in his thigh. He hadn't bothered to tell her what had happened. Not that she had asked. But still... No matter how much he claimed to love her, was this a man she could trust?

Emily kicked herself again over her own indecisiveness and lack of confidence. This was exactly why she wanted to get away from her father and her parents' house. She left and then what did she do? Fall for the first man who seemed to support her. She mistook love for control. Look what that had got her! Now, with Luke, she had to question what kind of man he was. She couldn't make the same mistakes again. Once was a mistake, jumping from one relationship to the next without being cautious was just plain stupid.

Ten years was a long time. He admitted to getting into bad trouble after she went to college. Now he talked about not letting her go. This sounded a lot like the other men in her life.

Still, Emily admitted to herself that she didn't have the full picture. She didn't know the details of Luke's life or why he got into a knife fight. The first order of business after she got the restraining order would be to sit down with Luke and get some straight answers.

But first things were first. She needed to deliver these sandwiches before they got too cold, then get herself to the courthouse and get in touch with her boss at one point today as well.

She found herself at Luke's apartment in no time, and bounded up the stairs, bag in hand. "Hey, Luke," she said as she opened the door. "I brought—" Emily entered the apartment and saw the back of a woman's head in the chair by the sofa.

"Emily," Luke said and made an attempt to get up before giving up. "This is the wife of one of my employees. Helen, this is Emily."

"Hi, Emily," said Helen, twisting in her seat. "Well, Luke. Thanks. I guess I should go."

"I won't keep Gibs too long at work tonight, Helen."

"Okay, thanks, Luke. I'll be in touch." As Helen walked by Emily she murmured, "It was nice to meet you."

"You, too." She didn't miss the concern and worry lines on Helen's face. What was going on? "Bye." When the door shut behind Helen, Emily sat down on the chair Helen had occupied and stared at Luke. "Can't keep the women away from you, huh?" She winked, trying to lighten the mood and erase the anxiety on Luke's face as well.

"Guess not. What's this?" He sniffed the bag Emily set on the table.

"Your breakfast. Bacon and egg sandwiches from the Walkerville Diner."

"Sounds awesome."

Emily dug into the bag and pulled out a sandwich. "The rest are yours."

"Rest?"

"I got two for you. I didn't know how hungry you were."

"Two sounds good. So what's our plan today?" He took a sandwich from the bag and settled into the couch. "I seem to recall you called your boss for the day off. Are you taking care of me? Offering a sponge bath?"

She shook her head and grinned at him. "Sorry, no sponge bath." The amusement left her face as she thought about what her plans were for today. "I have to go to the courthouse and file papers. Justin, he's my lawyer, told me it may take a couple hours, but they'll give me temporary orders and serve the papers to Evan while he's still in the courthouse."

Luke's breakfast sandwich froze halfway to his mouth. He slowly set it down. "What are you talking about? Did that idiot Evan do something else now?"

She hadn't told him about last night or yesterday morning. "I'm putting a restraining order against him. It's a temporary one now until I can get a proper one."

Luke's face burned red with anger. "What the hell happened? I'll kill him!"

"It's fine." It's my own fault. "He was waiting for me outside of work yesterday morning and then showed up at my house at the end of the day. I called my lawyer and he told me to wait in my car, not to go inside. So I didn't. Evan came out and caused a commotion which had the neighbors calling the police."

"I'll kill him." Luke grimaced as he pushed himself off the couch and reached for his leather jacket.

Emily put her hand on his arm. "Maybe save it for another day. I'm fine. Honest."

"Yeah, but I'm not. Neither will the douchebag when I'm finished with him."

"You going to hit him with your crutch?" She shook her head. "I will if I need to."

"You don't need to. Luke," she said sternly. "It's going to be taken care of. I need to let the law do its job. I want the case he has against me thrown out. This is the best way."

"He hasn't laid a hand on you, has he?"

She shook her head. "He's full of hot air." She checked her watch. "I need to get going so I can be there before the courthouse opens. Justin said the sooner the better."

"You'll be there while he is? I don't like that, Emily."

"I'll be perfectly safe. It's the courthouse, full of police and guards and stuff like that." Emily took another bite of her sandwich and slid what was left over to him.

"I'll go with you."

"No. You're supposed to be in bed. Why did you get up? Because of Helen?"

"I had a lot of visitors this morning."

"More than just Helen?"

"Just the stupid doorbell."

"How about you rest and don't answer the door anymore for today? Pretend you're sleeping."

"Only if you'll join me."

"In bed? Ahhh, then I'll never get that restraining order." She smiled. When she was around Luke, nothing seemed as bad as it was. It just sucked that her mind had her questioning everything when she wasn't with him. "I've got to get going, but when I get back we need to sit down and talk about things." Impulsively she bent down and kissed him, slipping her tongue into his mouth and then pulling back just as he responded. She liked his reaction. He groaned and tried to reach for her as she stepped away and picked up her purse.

"What things?" said Luke, but she was already out the door and avoided answering him.

The clerk's office was a small room with a bank of windows that faced the door. Behind the windows stretched rows of desks filled with people working at computers. Opposite the service windows sat a long counter with some stools. On that wall hung a long two-row rack where court forms were available. Emily stared around the room as she waited her turn.

The court clerk was very nice, though she was a little harried. Emily sat at a seat at a counter against the wall waiting for the woman to come back with the judge's signature. She looked at all the different forms and was glad she had Justin to fill out the paperwork for her court order.

Different people came and went filing various papers with the court. Checking her watch every five minutes, she grew anxious waiting. What if the judge denied the order? Maybe he would think her complaints weren't serious enough to warrant an order of protection. The clerk came several times to tell her that the Family Court docket was full today and she was still waiting for the judge to read Emily's application.

At lunchtime the clerk came out and told her the judge was taking a lunch and that Emily should grab some lunch too. She nodded and sighed. Justin had warned her it would take a while. Emily stepped out of the courthouse and called Luke. "Hey, this is taking longer than I thought. I can't get you lunch."

"That's okay babe. I'll order a pizza."

"Again?"

"Yeah, lunch of champions. No problem. I'll see you when you get here."

"How's your leg feeling?"

"It's fine. How're you?"

"Tired of waiting. Nothing I can do about it." She wondered if she should call her boss again. Maybe she should send Justin a text to get him to type up a letter to explain what had been going on. She could do that after lunch while she waited.

She grabbed lunch from a sandwich shop on Main Street. She hadn't eaten out this much in a long time. Evan never wanted to go out, and Emily would end up cooking for both of them. Not that he liked her cooking. He'd complain most nights about what she served for dinner. She shook her head. How had she put up with it? Or not noticed his lack of manners?

At two o'clock she headed back to the courthouse and resumed her wait. After another hour, the clerk waved her to the window.

"Okay, the judge signed the order. I'm going to type up the judge's order, copy this up and call the marshal to deliver it. I've checked and they haven't called your boyfriend's case yet so we still have some time. Just give me a few more minutes so I can give you your two copies."

"Thank you," said Emily. A feeling of relief settled around her and she finally felt like she could breathe.

The clerk looked at her with concern. "I'll be right back."

After a few minutes, a burly looking man in a marshal's uniform entered the clerk's office and the clerk came out of the office door. "Here," she said to the marshal. "He's in court right now. They just called his case."

"I'll go right down and wait for him to come out."

"Great, Henry. Thanks."

As the marshal exited the door he'd just come in from, the clerk turned to Emily. "These are your two copies. Keep one on you at all times so that you have it should he show up, and keep the other one in a safe place. Here also is your court date for the hearing. Show up on that date regardless of anything else. If you don't, the order of protection drops." The woman put her hand on Emily's. "I know how difficult this all is."

"You do?"

The woman nodded and she smiled sadly at her. "You are doing the right thing. Don't let anyone tell you that you aren't. Guys like this need something to stop them. They stopped listening to the women in their lives a long time ago. Here are some numbers for you. Don't hesitate to call any of them. Believe me, this is just the first step from getting out from under."

Emily blinked. "Th-Thank you. You've been very helpful."

"No problem. Good luck, Emily."

"Thanks." Emily walked out of the clerk's office to the elevator that would take her to the first floor. On the ride down she stared at the numbers. The first one was the number for the National Domestic Abuse Hotline. The second was a pamphlet for a support group for domestic violence victims.

Emily stared at them, shocked. She didn't consider herself a domestic violence victim. She just had a shitty ex-boyfriend who was trying to make her life miserable. Sure, Evan had gone too far, but he wasn't an abuser, was he?

She stepped out of the elevator, staring at the pamphlet, and nearly jumped back inside the closing door when someone screamed her name.

Chapter Twelve

A Turn for the Worse

Luke decided into the second slice of pizza that staying at home was a drag. He didn't normally watch television and there weren't any good sports games on. A short nap after all the visitors in the morning helped stretch out the day, but after Emily's call woke him, he couldn't get back to sleep. What would make him feel better was a good ride on his bike, but that wasn't happening any time soon. He was about to call the shop when there was some loud angry pounding on his door.

"What now?" thought Luke. "Just a minute!" he called out.

"Open up! Search warrant!"

"What the hell?" he thought.

"Give me a sec. I'm on crutches here."

Luke moved as quickly as he could to the door and tore it open. "What's going on?"

Detective Anglotti pushed a piece of paper toward his face.

"Search warrant," he growled.

"What's this about?"

"Step aside and let us in," said Anglotti. "Otherwise, we'll have to arrest you for obstruction."

Luke moved aside, gripping the hand rests of his crutches so tight his knuckles turned white. The two detectives and three uniformed officers entered his apartment and started tearing through it. It was a small apartment, just the kitchen, living room, bath and bedroom but they took their time as they opened every drawer, cabinet and closet. They tossed everything on the floor and rattled dishes. When they began to overturn furniture

Luke opened his mouth to say something but Anglotti turned and glared at him.

"Detective, I found this," said a uniformed officer coming from the bedroom holding the manila envelope Gibs brought him earlier. Anglotti opened it and whistled. "What's this? Three, four grand?"

"It's five grand," said Luke. "The employee I bailed out repaid the money I gave the bail bondsman."

"You must pay your employees well."

"Well enough. Is there any crime in having cash?"

"It is if it's money derived from selling drugs."

Luke set his jaw and stared at Anglotti. "I don't sell drugs, detective."

Everything Luke ever owned; books, pictures, and clothing were strewn on the carpet or floors of his apartment. The furniture was overturned and the pieces that were against the walls were pulled away.

"Find anything else," Anglotti said to the other officers. One by one they shook their heads.

"Maybe they'll find something at the business," one of the uniformed officers said.

"Wait. You're searching my business?"

"My partner is there now. Does that upset you?"

"It upsets me that you're disrupting my business."

"Oh, I plan on disrupting your business, Mr. Wade."

Rage burned through Luke and it took every ounce of control not to do something stupid that would land him in jail. "I don't know where you are getting your information, but my business is repairing bikes. Period."

"So you say, Mr. Wade. Our informants say otherwise."

"What informants?" growled Luke.

"Confidential informants, Mr. Wade. Come on, boys. We'll let Mr. Wade clean up the mess here."

Luke watched the officers walk out of his apartment. At the last minute Anglotti turned and flicked the manila envelope at Luke. It landed at Luke's feet."

"Enjoy your legal cash, Mr. Wade." Anglotti drew out the word 'legal' in a way that made it sound like it was anything but legal. Luke wanted to smash the manila envelope in his face. "You might want to put it to good use, like hiring a lawyer. You're going to need one." Anglotti slammed the door shut.

Luke stood in his entryway staring at the hell the police made of his home. He turned over the smallest chair, though it strained his sore leg when he put weight on it. He flopped into it, and winced. He pulled his phone out of his pocket but knew calling the shop would make things worse instead of better. Luke would have to wait until one of them called him.

He considered whether or not to call Emily, but considering what she was going through, he decided against it.

His phone rang. His shop's number displayed on his cell phone. With a mixture of relief and apprehension, he answered the call. "Hey."

"Hey, boss," said Gibs.

"How bad is it? The police were here and tore my apartment to shit."

"It's a little messy, but Saks and Pepper are straightening it up now."

"Good, after that's done, close up the shop and come over here and help me with my apartment. It's a total disaster."

"Sure thing, Luke. We'll be there as soon as we can."

Gibs and Saks showed up at the apartment, but Pepper begged off.

"What a fucking mess," said Gibs.

"Yeah," said Luke.

"Here," said Saks. "The time cards and the checkbook."

"Got any beer," asked Gibs. "It's been one helluva day."

Luke glared at him. "As far as I'm concerned you're still on the clock."

"Okay, fine," grumbled Gibs. He walked around the apartment and stuck his head in the bedroom door. "They didn't spare a thing, did they?"

"No," said Luke glumly. "What did they do at the shop?"

"Same thing, just there isn't that much stuff to go through," said Saks.

"On the other hand, boss," said Gibs with a grin, "all the inventory is nice and ordered now. Even found those items you thought was missing."

"You did the inventory?" Luke said in wonder.

"It was the least I could do," said Gibs.

"Pepper helped him."

"Besides, I didn't trust those cops," said Gibs.

"Yeah, I didn't either," said Saks. "What's going on, boss? We all know you're as straight as an arrow. Why would the cops think you're crooked?"

"They got some bad information. And I think it was from the Rojos."

"Rojos?" said Saks. "That Latin motorcycle club?"

"Gang is more like it." Luke shook his head. "This is fucking ridiculous."

"Why? Did a Rojos go after you?" Saks picked up a picture and went to hang it back on the wall.

"A bunch of years ago I was an associate with the Rojos."

Gibs nearly dropped a picture. "You?" he said in disbelief.

"I was young, stupid and had nowhere else to go. I was in foster care until I turned seventeen, and then, well, you're out. The Rojos let me crash in their clubhouse, and they liked me pretty well, or at least I thought they did. They recruited white members because sometimes a white face can go into a neighborhood that another color would draw interest from the police." He waved his hand, dismissing the past. "The chapter I hung with was mostly junkies. One morning I woke to find one of the brothers dead next to me. I caught a glimpse of my future right there and saw it wasn't a healthy one. I got my things and high tailed it out of the clubhouse.

"What I didn't know was that the police were getting ready to raid the club and that shit went down the same day I left. The president of that chapter thought because I left that day, I was the snitch who had turned them in. Nothing was further from the truth. But from what I know, he hasn't changed his thinking on that. Stupid. I know."

"Shit, Luke!" Saks shook his head.

"There's more. He put the word out on the streets that he was coming for me. I was a dead man if I hung around. That's when I joined the Navy. I didn't like the idea of following orders and going to sea, but from what I could see it was going to take me far from home and away from the gangs. I won't lie. It was a struggle for me. But I straightened my shit out, saved my money and learned you didn't have to be a criminal to get by in the world."

"Why," said Gibs, "in the name of all that's holy, did you come back to Connecticut?"

Luke shrugged. "I went all over the world, but when it was time to leave the Navy, the only place that felt like home was here. So I came back. Besides, I learned that while I was away Lil' Ricki, that club's president, rose to state leadership. But he got caught for moving drugs and got a jail sentence for twenty years, minimum. And since he told everyone that he wanted to get retribution himself, I figured I was mostly safe back here. Every once in a while some kid who wants to patch in gets a wild hair to earn points by trying to take me out." Luke sighed and crossed his arms over his chest. "So there. Now you know why a Rojos would want to come after me." He'd never told anyone and couldn't believe he'd just told the two of them in such a matter-of-fact, mature, way.

"Shit," said Gibs at the same time as Saks.

"You should have told us sooner," said Saks.

Luke shook his head. "If I did, that would make my business the club's business."

"It doesn't matter what you think, boss," said Saks. "Any business a member has is club business. If one of us stinks like shit, we all stink of shit."

Luke looked at Gibs, who turned a shade paler. "You're right," Luke said.

"Well, let's get this straightened up for you," sighed Gibs, refusing to say any more. Luke had just given him the opportunity to tell them what had happened and why he had been arrested. Instead, he had closed the door.

Gibs and Saks worked quickly to put everything right while Luke sat on the couch going over the time cards adding up the hours. The two of them started in the bedroom with putting the bed back together and putting clothes away. Luke could only imagine how that was going. His Navy days taught him to keep his closets and drawers neat, but he had no idea how those guys organized things at home. For Gibs, Luke imagined that Helen kept the house straight, while Saks was a bachelor.

It was fucked up what the police did.

Even the distraction of doing the payroll didn't quell the indignation and anger Luke felt towards the cops who invaded his home and his business. Maybe they were only doing their jobs, but they acted like assholes as they did it. The assumptions and innuendos about Luke's character burned him the most. That, and because deep inside, Luke knew he could have become that kind of man if he hadn't joined the Navy.

Saks moved to the kitchen and began putting the stuff in there away while Gibs ran Luke's sad excuse for a vacuum cleaner over the carpets.

"Damn," Gibs muttered when he turned off the vacuum. "The shop vac would have done a better job."

"I have that just for emergencies. The cleaning woman brings her own."

"Dude, this thing is an emergency. Hit the Walstore and get yourself a new one."

Luke grinned. Gibs had just been in jail and he figured a crappy vacuum was an emergency? "I've bigger things to worry about." Luke ripped two checks from the large business checkbook. He snapped it shut and stood using his good leg. He handed a check to Gibs while looking him square in the eye. "And speaking of bigger things, Okie called this morning."

"Okie?" said Gibs. "How's he doing?"

"He says he's good. But somehow he heard about my little encounter the other night. Says the Rojos that stuck me was bragging about it to his leadership."

Saks walked into the living room. "What was that?"

Luke kept his gaze on Gibs while holding out a check to Saks, who took it, then whistled. "Boss, that's too much."

"You've been holding down the fort. Consider it a bonus. Can you do me a favor and get my mail from the kiosk downstairs?"

"Sure, boss."

Luke tossed him his keys and Saks left through the front door. With the door firmly shut, Luke whirled and faced Gibs. "What the fuck is going on?" snarled Luke. "What the hell are you into that has the cops thinking I'm a part of?"

Gibs held his hands up. "Luke, I swear, all I know is that Aces asked me to pick up a package for him. I got pulled over on I-91 and it's been shit since then."

"Where did you get this package?"

"A bar in East Haven."

Luke sucked in a breath. "La Concha?"

"Yeah. How did..."

"Fuck! Gibs! That's the headquarters for the Hombres."

Luke swayed on his crutches.

"That Latin gang?"

"Yeah, the one that's all over Bridgeport, Waterbury, and Hartford. Fuck, fuck, fuck!" He began pacing on his crutches and nearly fell as he turned around.

"Luke, you look ready to pass out. Maybe you should sit down, man."

"Sit! Hell no! You sure? You sure it was Aces that sent you down there?"

"Of course. He talked to me on that last road trip."

"And you had no idea what you were picking up?"

"No, Luke. I swear. I was just doing the Prez a favor."

"Oh man. This is so fucked, you have no clue."

"Luke. Tell me what's going on." Gibs looked scared now and he had every right to be.

"No fucking wonder that kid was out for a piece of me the other night. The Rojos are the road knights for the Hombres, their shock troops, and their mules for transport. That someone in the Hombres is trying to branch out to other clubs, well, that's a gang war right there. And Hades' Spawn is in the fucking middle of it!"

Chapter Thirteen

Realizations

"Emily!"

There was a pause before her name was cried out again.

"Emily! How the hell can you do this to me?"

She looked up in shock to see Evan blocked by the marshal.

"Escort her out of here," barked the marshal to one of his buddies.

"Emily!"

"Sir. Calm down. You can't speak with her. There's an order of protection in place."

"Emily! Don't do this! You have no freakin' clue what you're doing!"

Another marshal came to her side. "Let's get you to your car."

"Emily, you fucking bitch! I'll get you." Evan pushed against the marshal, nearly knocking him down.

"That's it!"

Emily turned her head to see Evan spun around and handcuffed by the marshal. She looked away quickly, aware all eyes in the courthouse lobby were turned toward her. Her face flushed in her embarrassment and she kept her eyes to the ground, barely registering where they went until they were in the parking lot.

"Where's your car, Miss?" the marshal asked.

Emily looked up and pointed in the direction of her parked car. "He's arrested again, isn't he?"

"For now, though whether charges will be filed is another story. That was an unfortunate bit of timing when you came out of that elevator."

"I suppose it was. I'll be okay from here."

The marshal shook his head. "I'll make sure you get to your car."

"Thanks."

"And Miss, don't back down. No matter what your family or friends tell you, make that hearing."

"I will."

"Good luck."

Emily unlocked the car with shaking hands and got in. She started the car and opened the windows. She was in no condition to drive. Her heart hammered at a rhythm that made her legs want to run. To run away from Evan and hide. She stared down at the pamphlet still clutched in her left hand. She flipped open the folded over part with a trembling hand.

Dating Relationships

You may think that you aren't an abuse victim, especially if you are "only" dating someone. However, for most women the cycle of abuse starts in the dating relationship and many women downplay their partner's behavior as being intensely interested in them as a person. At first, your partner may be overly solicitous, even overly romantic in an effort to win you over. However, as the relationship continues abusive behavior crops up, sometimes in small ways, and the woman will do anything to bring the relationship back to the overly solicitous part of the relationship, even giving in on some points that she thinks is important. But over time, the abusive behavior escalates, and she finds herself in a pattern of making excuses and tolerating his bad behavior. At a certain point she may seek to change him, but that rarely happens. The woman is left confused at how such a wonderful man could turn on her.

Her eyes shifted and she read another part of the pamphlet.

Signs of Abuse:

Extreme jealousy or insecurity

Constant put-downs

Possessiveness or treating you like property

Telling you what to do
Constantly checking in on you
Explosive temper
Making false accusations
Isolating you from your friends and family
Preventing you from doing things you want to do
While not all abusers will display all these behaviors, if you see at least one of them you should be concerned that you may be in an abusive relationship.

Emily gulped. She recognized many of these behaviors in Evan. But what was worse, she recognized them in her father as well.

She set down the pamphlet and the orders of protection. She set the car in drive and began to ease out of the parking stall. But she stopped short, startled, when she heard knocking on her driver's side window. A man she did not recognize held out a badge and made a motion for her to lower the window.

"Emily Dougherty?"

"Yes."

"I'm Detective Anglotti with the Westfield Police."

Emily blinked. A million things ran threw her mind, but first and foremost she wondered if they released Evan. "What can I do for you, Detective?"

"You know Luke Wade?"

"Yes, sir."

The detective rolled his eyes. "'Sir,' that's good. Is that what they taught you in Catholic school?"

Emily felt her face flush. "What is this about, Detective?"

"I spent a little time at your boyfriend's house today, Ms. Dougherty."

"Is Luke okay?"

He rolled his eyes again and fished a business card out of his pocket and handed it to her.

"I'll give you props. You got that innocent routine down cold."

"What do you want?" She didn't understand why he was being so rude. The detective's manner scared and insulted her at the same time. Her heart hammered in her chest while she waited for him to speak.

"Your boyfriend's ass deep into some big shit, Miss Dougherty. I suggest that if you don't want to get arrested along with him you cooperate with us. Give me a call when you're ready to talk."

As the detective swaggered from her, Emily's breathing sped up, and she couldn't control it. She cupped her hands over her nose. It had been years since she had a panic attack, but this one ran over her like a freight train. Her heart hammered in her chest as she breathed in her own ragged breaths in an effort to gain control over her body. She grew lightheaded. She concentrated on taking deep breaths and slowly her heart and her breathing slowed. Shaking, she reached for her phone from her purse and called Justin. She didn't want to do it, but she had to. Everything that Angela and Justin told her was coming true. She should have stayed away from Luke. Emily had no idea what trouble he was in, but if detectives were involved it had to be bad.

Justin didn't answer so she left a message for him to call. She checked her phone. It was four in the afternoon. Angela would be up now. Emily decided to go see her sister.

"You did what!"

"Please don't yell, Angela," said Emily. "I spent the night with Luke. He was injured and in bad shape. The papers from the Emergency Room—"

"The Emergency Room!"

"Angela, please listen. They listed a number to call and the nurse said he shouldn't be alone. So I stayed."

"And how did you get to his apartment in the first place?"

Emily sighed and put her hands in her lap. "Angela, when you screw up your face like that, you look exactly like dad."

"What's that supposed to mean?"

Emily fished the pamphlet the court clerk gave her from her purse and handed it to Angela.

Her sister's eyes narrowed. "What's this?"

"Just read this section, Angela. The one that says, 'Signs of Abuse'."

Angela glanced over it quickly. "So?"

"Don't you see it, Angela? Dad is just like this."

"No, he's not, he's—"

"What? Protective? Cares about our welfare? Look at the list, Angela. He's always telling me what to do, shows up at my apartment checking into my business, loses his temper at the drop of a hat, and accuses me of things that I never do or ever did."

"That's you and him. He doesn't treat me like that."

"Doesn't he? When was the last time you did something he wouldn't like?"

"Well, I, well, hell, Emily why would I?"

"Yes, why wouldn't you? You saw firsthand what happened to little girls who don't listen to their father. So you made sure you didn't suffer the way I did. You made sure you were 'good' all the time. Maybe you weren't punished the same way I was, but you were a victim just the same."

"That's ridiculous. I'm not a victim."

"I didn't think I was either. But who did I pick at the first opportunity? Evan. And I think I did because he reminded me so much of dad."

"Emily, you cracked your nut. Evan's nothing like dad."

"Isn't he? Possessive, controlling, insulting, making false accusations. The list goes on, Angela."

"Dad never hit either of us."

"Evan never hit me either. And yet, I have to get an order of protection to keep him away."

"I can't believe you are saying these things, Em. Dad loves us."

"Evan told me he loved me too."

"It's not the same thing, Em, and you know it."

"Do I? All my life all I've done are things to please the men in my life and it's brought me nothing but heartache. Maybe it's just time I do the things I want to do."

"Emily, we're just looking out for you."

Emily looked at her sister and realized there was no way that she was going to change her sister's mind. "I appreciate that you are trying only to look out for my best interests. It's just too bad you don't know what they are."

"Emily, that's not fair."

"Yes, Angela. I think it is." She picked up her purse. "Tell Justin to give me a call when he gets a chance. There is something I have to talk to him about."

"What, Emily?"

"Just something between me and my lawyer."

Emily left her sister's apartment as fast as she could, even as Angela called her name. As her feet hit each step leading to the parking lot she moved farther away from her old life. Before, when she told her father off, she was reacting in anger. That was wrong. Luke was right. At some point she did have to grow up and make her own decisions.

But what would those decisions be? If she moved closer to Luke she risked involving herself in his problems, and they seemed to be very serious ones. Her own legal situation was not good, and just as Justin and Angela predicted, getting involved with Luke only made them worse.

When she thought of Luke, her heart melted. He truly loved her. Of this she had no doubt. What she did doubt was if that was enough to keep them together.

Chapter Fourteen

The Letter

Saks handed Luke his mail and he quickly shuffled through it until he found a handwritten letter. "Sit down, guys," he said. "I think this is something we all need to hear."

Saks grabbed a chair from the dining room table and Gibs sat on the lazy boy by the sofa. Luke ripped open the envelope and unfolded the sheet of paper inside.

Spade,

I started this chapter of Hades' Spawn when you were a sprout, but when I did it, I did it differently than how National wanted. I know I didn't talk much about National, and there is a good reason. Let's just say the heart of the organization when I left Arizona was closer to its namesake than how I built this chapter. I was at a place in my life where I was tired of the bullshit I went through in Tucson and I wanted something different. Maybe I just should have made up a new name, but there was a time when Hades' Spawn stood for something. I still had pride in the patch I got when I joined them. Things changed after that.

When the Tucson brother showed up at my door from the Arizona chapter, I had to let him in. He was a brother with the same patch. And he had a good story about how he was sick of the Tucson shit. Now I realize that I should have slammed the door in his face.

I've learned some things in here because that fuck Lil' Ricki can't stop shooting off his mouth. The jerk likes to annoy me, but he has good reason. I'm sure you've pieced some things together, and if you haven't yet, you soon will.

I won't say I don't deserve to be in here, because I did enough shit in my life to put me in this place ten times over. Maybe the time I serve here will put things right. I don't know. But what put me here now I had nothing to do with. I should have seen it coming.

So don't let anyone fuck you over. I'll need something to come back to when I'm out of here, and that will be my club.

See you when I see you.

Okie.

Luke folded up the letter and put it back in the envelope. Then he tore it into little pieces. Gibs and Saks watched him, grim looks on their faces.

"Did he just say what I think he did?" said Saks. "That Aces set him up?"

"Sure sounds like it and it makes sense."

"I find it hard to believe," said Saks.

"Listen up, Saks. Gibs, here, was arrested Monday night doing an errand for Aces. Now Gibs is on the hook for drug possession with intent to sell."

Saks sat back with a look of shock on his face.

"You still think Aces is a stand-up guy, either one of you?"

Gibs shook his head. "Not in my book."

Saks sighed. "This is some serious shit."

"It gets deeper. I think the reason why Gibs got pulled over is that some informant from the Rojos called it in. I think they did this because they don't want to get cut out of the Hombres drug business. Aces got us all in a ton of shit because he is trying to expand National's business in our territory. Right now, all of us are bulls-eyes for the Rojos."

"And you think Aces set up Okie because Okie was trying to stop him?"

"Yes. That is the only thing that makes sense."

"What are we going to do?"

"I'm not sure. This is bigger than the local cops can handle. Hombres and Rojos spread across many states."

"And we don't even have solid evidence," said Gibs.

"Yeah, cops can come up with their own innuendo and accusations, but they won't listen to other people's no matter how much sense it makes.

"Saks," continued Luke. "I want you to get on the phone tonight and make other arrangements to store people's bikes in the garage behind the store. Call the owners, and tell them we'll put them somewhere else for now, or they can pick them up."

"Why, boss?"

"Because any property on mine is subject to seizure by the government if they should make a case against me. I don't trust Aces and I don't want my customers out their property should he pull some shit on me."

"Okay, boss. I'll get right on it."

"Gibs, I want you to stay home. I'm shutting the business down so all of us can take a nice long vacation. You need to be the soul of discretion until your court case, so I don't want to see you anywhere but in your backyard or your house, no matter who calls you."

"Okay, Luke."

"Call me tomorrow, eh?"

"Sure."

"And thanks for helping me get this place straightened out."

"No problem," said Gibs.

"Anytime," added Saks.

"Now, hate to cut this short but I've got some thinking to do."

"Sure. Thanks, man," said Gibs.

"Later," said Saks.

"And don't talk to any cops, either of you. By tomorrow, I'll have representation and then the cops can go through the lawyer."

His employees left, leaving Luke alone with his thoughts. They were in a world of shit generated by a man who didn't understand the shady underpinnings of Connecticut gangs.

These thugs were among the most ruthless of all of the gangs. Killing leadership was done without hardly any provocation. Lil' Ricki must think himself lucky to have concrete walls and barbed wire between him and his club.

There was no way the Rojos would tolerate any club cutting in on their business. The problem was convincing the Rojos Hades' Spawn had no interest in doing that. And for that to happen, Aces, and possibly Wolf and Dagger, would have to be tossed from the club. The trouble was, for that to happen he'd have to get a consensus from the other members, and as far as he knew, they didn't have a clue about what was going on.

He pondered the problems putting bits together. Somehow, he'd have to get the Rojos and possibly the Hombres behind the idea that Hades' Spawn was no threat. But to do that he'd have to find out which Hombres member was looking to exploit the Spawn. Luke didn't like that idea at all. Poking into Hombres business was dangerous. But there was more than one danger than the Latin gangs. The police were a wild card, a threat as potent as the Rojos. He dialed his business lawyer.

"Stone," answered the lawyer.

"Hey, Matt. Luke Wade. I need a referral."

"What kind of referral?"

"A criminal lawyer. Know any good ones?"

"I know a couple."

"I need an appointment tomorrow."

"Okay, I'll make some calls for you."

"Thanks. And I need some changes to my will."

"Changes? Wait. What's going on Luke?"

"I want to make sure some people are taken care of."

Stone listened patiently as Luke outlined the changes in his will.

"Okay, I'll draft it and FedEx it to you for your signature."

"Great."

"I'll call you with the appointment."

"Thanks, Matt." Luke was under no illusions. He was playing with fire so hot he could go up in flames. The only other option he had was to run; leave his business behind and go somewhere else. But that would mean he'd forsake the life he built and the friends he made. And Emily? She was so deep into her family, she'd never leave them, and he wouldn't ask her to. Not that he didn't love her, but because he did. He couldn't ask her to leave everything and everyone she loved behind just for him.

Except Luke couldn't make that decision now. He just had to see if he could work things out. Leaving would be plan B if what he had in mind didn't work.

He looked at the time on his phone. It was well after four and he expected Emily back long before that. Luke dialed her number, but there was no answer. His anxiety shot through the roof now. He should have gone with her to make sure she was okay.

There was a knock on the door, and when he opened the door, Emily rushed in his arms. He barely got the door shut before she peppered him with kisses, then finally claimed his mouth.

She melted into him, holding onto his neck and thrusting her tongue into his mouth. Luke pushed her against the wall and his crutches fell away. He didn't know who was holding up whom but he didn't care. His hands travelled down to her perfect round cheeks and he grabbed them and crushed her hips into his. Her sleeveless dress had little buttons down the front so flimsy that he was able to pull them off with his teeth. Soon, the top of the dress opened and he attacked her breasts. He pulled away a second to slide the arm holes off her arms. Her chest heaved as he reached around and unsnapped her lacy bra, freeing the creamy globes. Luke buried his face in her chest, loving her scent and the softness of her skin. He gripped one breast from underneath and squeezed it, popping her pink nipple forward. He fell on the tender flesh, sucking the nipple into his mouth. She arched her back and pressed her hips into his erect shaft. They both groaned together, and Luke rubbed his cock against her mound.

"Oh fuck, Luke."

Her hands fumbled on the waistband of his shorts, and Luke took a free hand to push them down. Then he pulled at her flimsy thong and yanked, tearing it off her.

"Luke! Those were expensive."

"I'll buy more," he growled. "Turn around."

Emily faced away from him.

"Put your hands on the wall," he ordered in a sexy voice. As she did, he reached for her folds and found them drenched. At his discovery, he pressed his cock between her butt cheeks. "Want me?" he whispered. His heart hammered in his chest. Luke's worry for her during the day flamed his desire for her to wild and unstoppable heights.

"Yes," she whispered hoarsely.

He didn't have to ask. He knew it, but he liked hearing her say it. With his hands he pinched her nipples hard until she drew a sharp breath. "I can't wait to have you," he said as he pressed harder against her. "And I'm not going to."

"Then don't." She moaned, her fingernails scraping along the wall.

"Spread your legs."

He lined his shaft to her channel and sunk in slowly. Emily gasped as he slid into his balls. "Ready?" He knew she was.

"Fuck me."

Luke didn't have to be told twice, but the way she swore at him, he couldn't stop himself. He pressed his shaft back and forth, the intensity of his thrusts rising.

Emily trembled against him. "Harder," she gasped.

He sunk himself into her over and over, his need for her a runaway train. He grasped her around the waist and pulled her toward him roughly, laying his head against her back. He could hear her heart pounding, and her channel clenched, as her heat and her wetness pulsed around him.

Emily gave a strangled cry. "Again. Again," she repeated as he throbbed inside of her.

Fire lit Luke at her words and he pulled out and shot his load, painting her back in white streaks. "Oh, fuck."

"What?" Emily looked over her shoulder, her eyes half closed as she panted.

He turned her around pressed his lips against hers. "I wasn't wearing a condom, baby."

Her eyes flew open. "Crap. I wasn't thinking."

"I did, baby. I always put you first. Always."

"Well, you better, because my wardrobe isn't going to last long like this." She grinned and rotated her hips against him.

Luke leaned against her, thinking that all he needed was her next to him always. He sighed. He didn't know how that was going to work out.

She ran her fingers in his hair. "What's going on, Luke? Are you okay? Is your leg hurting?"

"I suppose." He wasn't thinking about his leg. "Em?"

"Yes, Luke?"

"We have to talk."

Chapter Fifteen

Confessions

Wrapped in Luke's robe after she had taken a shower, Emily sat down on the bed where Luke lay stretched out. He had propped pillows behind him and made a spot for her beside him.

"How's your leg doing?"

"Sore," he said, "but I'll live."

"You were doing a bit more than that a few minutes ago." She tried to sound stern but the corners of her mouth kept twitching upward.

Luke smiled, but it was etched with worry. He moved his hand over hers, holding it lightly. "How did things go at court? Did you get the restraining order or do I need to have a little talk with your ex?"

She liked his tough guy approach. Evan didn't stand a chance against Luke, even with a hurt leg. "Good. I got the order."

"I'm glad."

"It took forever and then when Evan saw me, he went off. They had to arrest him again."

"Even better." Luke's brows crushed together. "He didn't hurt you did he?"

She shook her head. "There was a marshal holding him back. Evan didn't stand a chance." She decided not to tell him about how shaky she was after and how another marshal had to walk her to her car. Nor did she mention the pamphlet and her realization about her father. She would deal with each thing in steps. "What about you?" She glanced around. "It looks like you cleaned up the place. You were supposed to be resting."

Luke gave a shrug of his shoulder. "It was a busy day. That's what I need to talk to you about." He took a deep breath. "The police searched my apartment today."

Emily looked down at his hand holding hers. "Why'd they do that?"

"Because they believe, with good reason, that members of Hades' Spawn are running drugs."

"Are you involved with drugs, Luke?" She couldn't believe she'd asked him straight out.

"No." He looked at her in surprise, but continued. "However, I found out that some of our members are."

Emily pursed her lips and looked at the wall. Everything Angela and Justin said was coming true. "Is there more to this?"

"Yes."

"Then you shouldn't tell me. When I was at the courthouse a detective stopped me at my car. He said some nasty things, Luke, and he seems to believe you're involved with drugs and that I know all about it."

Luke pushed his body up to a sitting position. "What? Which detective? Do you remember his name?"

She shook her head. "But he gave me his card." She stood and got her purse and dug through it till she found the card. She handed it to Luke.

"Anglotti," hissed Luke.

"You know him?"

"He's the asshole that tossed my apartment today."

"Tossed? Everything looks perfectly neat."

"That's because I had a couple of my employees help me straighten it out. Believe me, everything was thrown around. Everything."

"Oh, Luke."

"It's annoying. But what really pisses me off now is that he's bothering *you*."

"My lawyer told me that associating with you weakens my case." She figured she didn't have much of a case left to fight after Evan's outburst, but her charges with driving had nothing to do with Evan so she had to be careful.

"He's right."

"What're we going to do?"

"Emily, I have to do some things..." He ran his fingers through his hair, his face more serious than she had ever seen. "Some dangerous things to straighten this out. It might be best if we don't see each other for a while."

A sob caught in her chest. "I don't want to do that," she whispered.

"I didn't want to say it. But you were right to stop me from telling you what's happening. The less you know, the less the police can find out from you."

"This is so messed up." She fought tears forming in her eyes.

Luke reached and wrapped his arms around her. She laid her head on his shoulder. "Why does this have to be like this?" A tear slid down her cheek but she ignored it. "Why can't we just be happy together? God must have it out for us."

Luke kissed her neck.

"Baby. I'm no expert on God, but pretty much what I've seen tells me that it's people who screw with each other, not God."

She settled under the crook of his arm. She thought about what he said. It felt like high school all over again, except this seemed to hurt a lot more. She finally had the courage to start making her own decisions in her life and it was as if life didn't want them to be together. "I suppose you're right. People have been messing with us since we met. And now..."

"Hey, hey!" Luke lifted her chin. "The only ones that matter are you and me."

Emily bit her lip. "I want it to be like that."

"No good thing is easy, Em. We just have some challenges to overcome."

Emily sighed. "I don't think we will ever have things easy for us."

Her phone rang. She ignored it and then thought she'd better check it. She reached over Luke to get her purse on the nightstand. It was her lawyer. "Hi, Justin."

"Hey. I got your message. What's up, Emily?"

"I got the restraining order."

"That's good."

"But when I left the courthouse a police detective stopped me in the parking lot. He made some nasty accusations implying that I'm involved with drug running."

"What the heck? Where would he get that idea?"

"Guess, Justin."

Justin was silent for some long seconds. "Are you still seeing Luke Wade?"

"I'm at his apartment now."

"Emily—"

"You don't have to worry. Luke and I have been talking. We've both agreed we can't see each other for a while. Or till at least everything smooths over."

"Good. That's a smart decision."

"I just wanted you to know what happened."

"I'm glad you did. If Evan shows up or tries to contact you again you give him my number. After you call the police."

"I will."

"Are you going to be home soon?"

"Not tonight, Justin."

Justin was quiet again. "Are you sure?"

"It's what's going to happen. Goodnight, Justin." Emily clicked off the call.

"Are you sure you want to stay?"

"I want every moment I can get Luke, especially since I don't know when I'll see you again. I'll tell you this; it won't be another ten years." She put her phone down and put her arms around

Luke's neck. She buried her face in his chest, breathing in deeply. Damn, he even smelled sexy. "If I had a choice, I'd never leave you again." They were right for each other, no matter what the rest of the world thought.

Luke chuckled. "Say that when we are eighty, gray and getting around in walkers."

"As long as you chase me with that walker, I wouldn't care."

"I'll do more than chase you. I'll catch you."

"Not if I don't catch you first." Emily leaned into Luke hard, catching him off guard. He fell back onto the bed with a grunt. She attacked him with swift hungry kisses starting with his neck and working her way down his body. Luke's skin was delicious after the sex they just had. It was salty and musky, especially when she dipped lower on his torso.

His belly button earned special attention and he started laughing.

"Mercy! Uncle! Help! I'm being attacked by an insatiable woman!"

"Ticklish, 'eh? Complain all you want, Luke Wade," Emily said sternly. "You've had your way with me. Now I'll have mine with you."

His face turned sexier as he stared at her. "Oh, has my good girl turned bad after one day in the courthouse?"

"Maybe I'm good, or maybe I'm bad, or maybe it's good to be bad."

"How can I know?" He smiled.

"I guess we'll have to see," she said with a sly smile on her lips. Emily continued her downward trip, bringing her lips to Luke's hardening shaft.

"Uhhmm," he said appreciatively. "That feels good."

Emily gave his flesh a long lick. "Tastes delicious."

"It gets better," he says.

"Says you. I'll have to see for myself."

"I didn't, ah, know you were such a Doubting Thomas." His voice hitched as she licked the underside of his head.

"You know what they say," said Emily between licks. "Experience is the best teacher."

She covered the tip of his cock with her mouth. As the head slipped past her lips she became intoxicated with the feel of his hardening rod in her mouth. As she tongued the salty skin it grew rigid. His velvet skin felt like encased steel as she sucked him in, enjoying the taste and feel of his pulsing flesh. It touched the core of her to have such a direct effect on this sexy man. *My man*, she told herself.

He groaned. "Fuck, Emily. What you do to me."

"Mmmm," she mouthed and his dick twitched in her mouth. She hummed again letting the vibrations flow on the rod she sucked.

"Oh fuck!" he moaned.

Encouraged, Emily nibbled on the underside of his cock and down to his balls. Here his scent was even more intoxicating, she could barely breathe. Her clit tingled and her own moisture slicked her folds. On an impulse she sucked in one ball, taking in the succulent globe, while massaging his cock with her hand.

"Suck it, babe," he breathed raggedly. "Damn, oh fuck, don't stop."

Emily had no intention of stopping. The desire to please him filled her, and she forgot about herself as she concentrated on his pleasure. Her heart opened wide, loving how his cock throbbed to the beating of her heart. She wanted nothing more than to give him all the love she had. This act, which at other times and with other men seemed mean and crass, became the single fulfillment of all she held in her heart for him.

For so many years they were apart, and every single day, compared to this moment, felt empty and hollow. Her heart became a glowing ember ready to burst into flames.

She took his cock into her mouth as far as she could take it and he writhed under her. Luke muttered things she couldn't hear as she was concentrating so hard giving him everything she could. She rocked back and forth, groaning around his hard male heat, frenzied with the desire to make him come.

His fists beat the bed as if he was trying to hold something back and she sucked even harder.

"Oh hell, Em. You gotta, I'm going, oh shit." He vainly tried to push her shoulders away and off him, but she was a woman on a mission. She wrapped her fists around the base of his throbbing dick slicked with her spit and moved them in concert with her mouth.

That did him in.

His back arched as he pushed her head down onto him as his first shot flew down her throat. Yes! Luke's release brought a triumph that excited her more than any sex she had in her life. As he throbbed, giving all of himself to her, she brought her hand to the sensitive source of her own fire. She stiffened and her nipples became hard nubs that tingled without being touched. A thousand sparks engulfed her body as she thought she would explode. Was that even possible?

Finally, they both stilled and Emily rested her head against him with Luke's cock still in her mouth.

"Baby," said Luke, raising his head. "Are you okay?"

Emily raised her head, letting go of his softening manhood and smiled. "Never better."

His eyes widened when she spoke. She smiled again, realizing he hadn't expected her to swallow. "Come here," he said, reaching out his arms to her. She moved off his body and up his side to nestle in his arms. "Baby, you are so very good when you are bad."

"Good," Emily said. "Now it's your turn to show me how good you are being bad."

The early morning light splashed through the blinds on the bedroom windows. Emily got up as quietly as she could and dressed in jeans and a shirt she packed in her overnight bag.

"Hey," said Luke sleepily. "Where're you going?"

"I've got to get ready for work. I didn't bring any work clothes with me." She was supposed to call her boss yesterday and with everything completely forgot to.

Luke sat up and rubbed his face with his hands.

She bent over, kissed him and scrunched up her nose. "Your beard feels like sandpaper."

"Good. I want you to feel it when I kiss you."

"Oh, I feel it." She closed her eyes as she rubbed her cheek against the roughness. "I don't know if I can leave you. I feel like I just found me because of you."

"It's just for a little while."

"That's what Romeo thought when he said goodbye to Juliet."

"I'm not Romeo. For one thing, I'm older, and the second, I have an iPhone. Makes communication a whole lot easier."

"Oh yeah?"

"When you see a blocked call, it'll be from me." He stared up at the ceiling a moment. "Should things get real dicey, here..." Luke pulled out a piece of paper from his desk drawer and wrote down an email address and a password. "That's my qmail account. I don't use it much. If you don't hear from me, check the drafts file in my email. I'll leave you a message there."

"That's sounds cloak and dagger. Where did you learn this?"

"From a television show," he said with a shrug. "You feel free to do the same thing if there is something you want to tell me, but don't think you can say over the phone."

"You expect things to get real bad, don't you?" She shivered. All of a sudden it seemed too real. Like there was real danger. Not a fairytale ending.

"I just don't know, Emily. It's good to have a backup plan. First and foremost I want you safe. If you have any problems, call this guy."

Luke wrote a name, Saks, and a phone number on the same piece of paper.

"Who's he?"

"One of my employees. I'll be keeping in touch with him."

"Okay." Emily took the piece of paper. If she stayed any longer, she would never leave. Tears filled her eyes. "I have to go, Luke."

"One last kiss," he whispered, standing.

She smiled, a tear slipping down her cheek. "It better not be our last kiss."

"Okay. Last kiss for now." Luke wiped the single tear and pulled her hard to him. He crushed his mouth on her lips.

Emily's knees got weak under her, making it difficult to pull away.

Luke finally broke the kiss and swatted her butt. "Out, before I throw you back on the bed."

"Gosh. You just make it so hard to resist you." She smiled despite the depression hanging heavy in her heart. She was terrified this might be goodbye.

Chapter Sixteen

Mrs. Diggerty

Emily sat in the chair in front of Mr. Hobson's desk waiting for his response to what she just told him.

"Miss Dougherty, I can't have this kind of thing interrupting this office."

"I agree. I took steps yesterday and got a protective order."

"No, I mean you've lost so much time already, I think—"

"Mr. Hobson, before you say anything else, you might want to call my lawyer." She slid Justin's card across the desk to him. "He'll explain that Connecticut has employment laws that protect a domestic violence victim. It's required by law that you give me any court time needed to protect myself."

"Connecticut is an 'at will' state."

"I know that Mr. Hobson. But there are protections for employees like me. I hope you understand. For too long I haven't done the right thing to protect myself. Now it's time I do."

"I can appreciate that, Miss Dougherty. But I'm afraid I've made up my mind. Security will stand by your desk while you clear out your things and then escort you out."

"What?" This wasn't happening! She pictured a completely different scenario in her head.

"Don't make this harder than it has to be. If you don't want to cooperate I'll have security escort you out directly and I'll send your things to you."

"Mr. Hobson, you can't do this! The law says you can't do this."

He looked at her sternly. "I suggest then that you talk to your lawyer. Good-bye, Miss Dougherty."

His phone rang and he picked it up, swiveling in his seat facing away from her.

Emily rose on shaky legs and went to her desk. She sat there staring at her computer screen as cold shivers ran down her body. It was inconceivable that despite the law Mr. Hobson fired her.

"Miss."

Emily looked up to see a security guard standing beside her cubicle.

"You have to leave, Miss."

"Yes," she said. She still didn't move.

"Do you need help with your things?"

She shook her head and looked at her cubby. Emily didn't keep much there. There was a picture of her and her family and a calendar. She didn't care about the calendar. It was something she got for a grab bag gift at Christmas. When she opened the drawers of her desk, she found a few small personal items. Again, these weren't important but she put them in her purse anyway. She picked up the picture.

"I guess that's it," she said quietly. Emily rose and walked toward the front door. The people she worked with for the past five years didn't even look at her. It was as if she didn't exist. The guard opened the door for her.

She barely realized when she left the building until she stood beside her car.

"Are you okay, Miss? Do you want me to call someone?"

"He fired me."

"Yes, Miss."

"He shouldn't have done that."

"You should leave now."

"Yes, of course." Emily unlocked the car and sat in it. The guard stepped back as she started the car automatically and drove slowly out of the parking lot in a state of shock. The spring day was bright and sunny, but she didn't notice. Swinging onto the highway was done without thought. Likewise, she didn't realize it when she made it home or how long she sat in the car before she finally got out. Emily had never been fired from a job in her life. The way she was raised, getting fired meant that you did something shamefully wrong. Was it her fault Evan turned into a first-class jerk? Was it her fault she had to get a court order to keep him away? She'd made mistakes along the way, but she had been a completely competent worker until the past few weeks of hell when everything had exploded.

The sun shone overhead, and the inside of the car grew hot. Emily was not used to being outside on a workday. The street sat empty of cars reminding her that everyone but her was already at work.

She couldn't help it. Even though her mind told her she had done nothing wrong, inside her gut she felt the rare bitterness of failure. Everything she worked for since she left Walkerville to go to college, after leaving Luke, came to nothing. Going to school, getting her CPA license, and getting this job, all of that work dissolved like a puff of smoke.

She couldn't imagine what her father or mother would say. All her life her parents drummed into her that achievement was the only option. Failure was for lazy people or losers. But Emily's failure had nothing to do with how hard she worked for what she achieved.

Emily couldn't make sense of this in her mind. And worse yet, she couldn't lean on the one person she could trust with her feelings. Luke was in trouble, bad enough he had to keep her away from the danger of being with him.

She trembled with emotions roiling inside that threatened to burst out from her, carving her gut into a million pieces. Alternately she wanted to crawl into her bed and never get up or she wanted to hit something. Instead, tears of frustration and sadness rolled down her cheeks and she wiped them away with her hands.

"Emily?"

The rapping on her driver's side window sent an electric jolt of alarm through her.

"Emily, what are you doing home, dear?"

She blinked, relieved it was Mrs. Diggerty and opened the window.

"What're you doing down here, Mrs. Diggerty?"

"I just got back from shopping and saw your car."

"Oh, here. Let me help you."

"That would be wonderful, Emily. But, dear, why are you crying?"

"I lost my job today." Her face colored from embarrassment.

"Oh," Mrs. Diggerty said. "Well then, dear, you're very fortunate to find out now what idiots they are. Anyone who'd let you go would have to be. You'll find a better job with people who appreciate you."

"But I won't be able to make my rent."

"Emily, dear. I'm too old to sweat the small stuff. The good Lord will make sure it all works out in the end."

After Emily helped Mrs. Diggerty put away her groceries, the older woman insisted that she sit and have a cup of tea. Emily didn't want company but at the same time, her landlady was being so sweet and considerate, she couldn't tell her no.

"Now," said Mrs. Diggerty. "Tell me all about it."

"Being fired?" Emily said surprised.

"Of course."

"They let me go," Emily whispered as she stirred a teaspoon of sugar in her tea.

"Well, yes. But why?"

"Because of all the trouble I'm having with Evan. I had to go to court yesterday to get a restraining order to keep him away and miss a day of work. That, with the other days, well, he had enough."

"Really? What a dick!"

"Mrs. Diggerty!" Emily smiled, despite how sad she felt. No Luke. No job. No anything she valued left in her life.

"What? You think you young people own the corner on swear words?"

"No. I just never expected to hear any from you." It wasn't really a swear word but she wasn't about to tell Mrs. Diggerty that.

"Well, I call them like I see them. Someone once told me that you don't live to work, you work to live."

"They did?"

"Yes. That was when I was having trouble at my own job. That was in the sixties before all the changes and before I met my Ron. I had this boss—" She shivered as she said that. "You heard the expression Roman hands and Russian fingers? Well. That was him. And in those days they didn't have laws against sexual harassment. A girl had to put up with some of that to keep her job. And if she couldn't handle her boss, it was her fault. One day he was so bad, well, I left and I didn't go back. I had to move back in with my parents, which was awful because I was so proud I could support myself.

"Back then if you quit your job for any reason you could forget about unemployment insurance. I got another job eventually, but it was the same thing all over again. By then I had met Ron, so when he proposed I quit my job. He didn't mind. He was glad I could take care of things at home. I worked with him to build his business and we did all right. But I always felt bad that I gave up. I shouldn't have had to quit either of my jobs because men didn't know how to behave themselves."

"Wow, I guess I didn't know how far we've come."

"Have we, Emily? I wonder. You shouldn't have to worry about jerks like your ex-boyfriend and bosses who have no compassion or understanding. It just seems like the same old shit, different day, as Ron used to say."

"Well, what're we supposed to do?"

Mrs. Diggerty leaned into the table. "Don't give up. Don't ever give up. Dig in your heels and give it back to them. No one is going to stand up for us if we don't." She leaned back into her chair again. "But who am I to say? I certainly didn't put in the good fight."

"I wouldn't be too hard on yourself. It couldn't have been easy. I can't imagine having to put up with a boss with Roman hands and Russian fingers."

With Mrs. Diggerty's assurances that Emily could slide a couple months on her rent if she needed, Emily headed back to her apartment. Reger ran up to her meowing his displeasure at her absence.

Grabbing up the tabby, she shut her door behind her then walked to the kitchen to get a cat treat. "You," she said as she pulled the envelope of cat treats from the shelf, "are the most—"

She stopped when she turned toward the living room again and saw the word 'bitch' scrawled across the back of her door in red spray paint.

Emily shrieked and dropped Reger. He yowled when he hit the floor and then flew off to hide behind the couch. All of a sudden she couldn't breathe. She set her hands on her knees, her chest heaving in ragged gasps. "No! No! No! He got into my apartment?"

Terrifying images flashed through her mind like a freight train as she grew more light-headed from breathing too fast.

"How do these things happen?" she whispered out loud. "I have the order of protection." The law's supposed to protect me. "Why isn't it protecting me?"

She grabbed a paper bag and held it open over her nose trying to get control of her breathing. When finally it slowed, she stumbled to the couch and sunk down. She stared at the nasty red letters that violated her apartment. Taking her cell phone from her purse she dialed 911.

It took forever for the Walkerville Police to show up at her apartment. By the time they were done questioning her she felt like she had committed a crime. The order of protection didn't seem to impress them. Her either, at this point.

There were two cops, a younger one and an older one. The younger one seemed more sympathetic than the older man, but in the end it did little good.

"We're sorry, ma'am," said the younger man. "There just isn't any evidence that Mr. Waters broke in and entered your apartment."

"Are you sure you didn't give him a key?" asked the older one with a sneer.

She shot him an angry look. "I never gave him a key to my apartment."

"There's no sign of forced entry, so whoever it was had to have a key."

"No one has a key but my landlady."

"Then I suggest you change your locks." The older man headed outside.

The younger policeman handed her his business card before they left. "If anything else happens, give us a call." He looked at the word before shaking his head. "Maybe a fresh can of paint..."

"Sure," said Emily, feeling like the whole thing was a waste of time. She flopped onto her couch feeling more powerless than ever before.

She called Justin, but was forced to leave a message. Angela would still be asleep and she didn't want to call her parents. Emily stared at Luke's number on her phone, knowing she shouldn't call him. Yet he was the one person in the world she wanted to speak to right now. Maybe this once, it wouldn't be bad. They had only just said goodbye this morning. Not that long ago, really.

The line rang and rang and finally went to voice mail. "Luke, call me. I really need to speak to you."

Chapter Seventeen

The Deal

Luke sat in the office of the lawyer Matt Stone referred him to. He had told him the entire story, everything he knew and suspected. Torres listened to him carefully until Luke stopped speaking.

Carey Torres pressed his fingers together and stared at Luke thoughtfully. "Well, Mr. Wade…"

"Luke, please."

"Luke, I agree, some sort of informant was involved. And most likely he was given something for his testimony. This gives a lot of incentive to the informant to come up with something the police can use, whether or not it's truthful. However, there's nothing I can do until the police arrest you."

"I understand that. I want to retain you anyway. Here's five thousand dollars in cash."

"Cash? Is there anything I should know about this money?"

"I'm beginning to wonder. The police who searched my house left it behind."

"In the absence of any evidence."

"Yes, but with the biggest asshole cop I've ever met, that wouldn't have stopped them if he wanted."

"Where did you get this cash?"

"My employee paid me back for the bond money I put up. He said he got it from his savings."

Torres shrugged. "I'll tell you what. I'll have my secretary write you a receipt, and I'll keep this in my safe and we'll see how things play out."

"I'd appreciate that."

"If the police call on you again, I want you to do these things. If they ask you questions, say: I'll remain silent. I want to talk to my lawyer." He waited for Luke to nod. "No matter how many questions they ask say the same thing. Give them no information. Second, if they come to search your house, or business, say: I do not give consent to this search. Even if they have a search warrant. Search warrants are very specific documents that often define the limits of the search. If they go beyond their search parameters then they can't use what they find in a search. And just to be clear, they'll take anything that makes it look like you were involved in a crime."

"Good to know."

"And if they detain you for any reason, call me day or night. I have an answering service that will call me if a client's been detained or arrested."

"Thanks. I've got something else. These bastards are bothering close friends. My girlfriend was harassed when she was at the courthouse doing some business there."

"They'll do that. If what you think is true happened, they'll try to get information from anyone you know."

"She's in a bit of legal trouble and they pressured her with that."

"Yeah, they'll do that. It doesn't mean much unless they arrest her. Does she have a lawyer?"

"Yes."

"Then she'll have to work with him if something comes up."

"I see. Okay, then I won't take up any more of your time."

"It's a pleasure doing business with you. Now I want you to do one thing."

"What is that?"

"Stay out of trouble."

Luke nodded. "I think I can do that." As he walked back to his bike he checked his phone and blinked when he saw a call from Emily. He dialed her number immediately. "Emily. What's up?"

"Oh, Luke. It's awful. I lost my job today and on top of that, Evan got into my apartment and spray painted the word 'bitch' on my door. The police won't do anything. They say there's no proof." Emily's words tumbled out so fast it took him a minute to make sense of it all.

Luke's free hand clenched into a fist. "Did you call your lawyer?"

"Yes. He hasn't returned my call yet."

"Take a pic of what he did. Then go pack your things, enough for a week or so."

"But Luke—"

"No buts. You're going someplace safe, and right now that's not your apartment."

"I don't have anywhere to go that Evan can't find me."

"I'm sending a friend of mine to pick you up. His name's Saks."

"From your shop?"

"Yes. You stay with him until I come to get you, and that won't be until later tonight or maybe tomorrow. But whatever you do, you stay inside his house."

"Okay."

She sounded scared. He hated that. "I'll see you later. I'll take care of it."

"I love you, Luke."

"Love you too. Later."

It had been almost a decade since Luke drove to the Rojos clubhouse, but it seemed to have changed very little. The grand clubhouse of the Rojos was a dull yellow and aging trailer set on a piece of farmland on the edge of Westfield. It sat square in the middle of the property on top of a small hill. This position gave the people in the trailer an advantage in seeing down the long rutted path that led to the trailer. Luke never found out who owned the property. At the time he lived here it wasn't important.

Gibs drove behind him on the road of hard packed earth. If there was gravel on this grade at one time, it wore away long ago.

Luke pulled up a hundred yards from the trailer, and Gibs stopped behind him. They both let their engines idle.

"You sure you want to sit this close, Luke?"

"We stepped into the range of fire long before we drove onto this property, Gibs," said Luke as he wiped his palms on his jeans. "Hold up your hands, Gibs." Luke held up his own and looked at the ramshackle trailer. "We're unarmed," he shouted.

Gibs swore under his breath.

There was no movement seen in the trailer.

"Are you sure they're here, Luke?" asked Gibs. "I don't see their bikes."

"They keep them out of sight. There's a dip in the land behind the trailer. That's where they park them."

"Estamos desarmados," Luke shouted.

"Que quieres?" called a voice from the trailer.

"Quiero hablar!"

"Fuck this," muttered Gibs.

"Steady, Gibs," said Luke.

"Acerca de?"

"Cómo podemos ayudar a los demás."

The door to the trailer burst open and a wiry Puerto Rican slammed his way out of the trailer. He stared hard at Luke. "What makes you think you can do anything for us."

Luke took in the man's patches on his denim cut. The usual cross and triple six patch decorated the area over his heart, as well as a thirteen patch and set of black and white wings. The cut telegraphed the man's name, Sal, and rank, President. Behind him was the kid who knifed him at the Red Bull.

"That's him, Sal," the kid said.

Sal stared at Luke's patches.

"Spade, blanco?"

"I call 'em like I see them."

"Ah, well what I see is a ghost that shouldn't be here, citizen."

"True, I don't belong to such a worthy criminal organization such as yours, Sal. But our interests have merged."

"Cómo?"

"Someone in the Hombres is looking to cut you out of the business by bringing in my club to handle it. I don't like that idea. I'm sure you don't either."

Sal laughed. It was an ugly sound.

"Our brothers wouldn't do that to us, cabron. Get the fuck off our land."

"Wait. My brother here was at La Concha. He picked up a package there. Ask him about it."

Sal scowled. "I should cut out your tongue. I might before I'm done. You," he said, pointing to Gibs. "What did you see?"

"I met an older guy, in his fifties maybe. White beard. People called him 'Wiz' or 'Wizard'."

"That don't mean nothing."

"Does it mean something that he handed me a two-brick package of heroin?"

The Rojos face went from surprise to flushing red.

"You're lying."

Gibs crossed his arms against his chest. "My arrest by the police says otherwise."

"Sarmanbiche!" spit Sal.

"They're lying, Sal," said the kid behind him.

"Shut up!"

"But, Sal."

"I said, close your trap!" To underscore his point, Sal whirled and smashed the kid in his face with his hand.

Gibs chuckled behind Luke.

"What're you laughing at?"

"Let's not get off track, Sal," said Luke. "We have the same problem. I have no desire to get in the middle of Rojos and Hombres business."

"And what do you want to do about it?"

"You attack your problem from your end. I'll fix mine on this end. It's as simple as that."

"It ain't simple, ese. You can say what you want, but I need something more solid to take it to the higher-ups."

"What do you want?"

"The abombao Hombre that's part of this. Deliver him and I can do something."

Luke looked hard at Sal. "So what I'm telling you isn't news."

"People talk. So far I haven't listened."

"And now?"

"I think there's been enough talking."

Luke and Gibs pulled into the parking lot of the Westfield Diner and parked their bikes side by side.

"You sure you want to do this, man?" Gibs asked as they entered the diner. It was called a diner but looked more like a restaurant. Though there was a long counter to the back, booths filled the walls, and tables took up the floor. A bunch of people looked to the door to the two men wearing their club jackets. Luke took off his reflective sunglasses. Gibs kept his on.

"Yes. It's a good public place. The bastard won't try anything here."

A waitress greeted them.

"We'd like a table," said Luke.

Seated, they ordered coffee.

"Can I get you anything else," the waitress asked.

"No, thanks. We're waiting for someone."

Gibs slowly stirred sugar into his coffee. "I thought you said that your lawyer told you to keep out of trouble."

Luke sipped his black coffee. "He did."

"And you're ignoring good advice you paid for?"

"This trouble we should've cleared up months ago." He was still trying to figure out how everyone had missed it.

Gibs shook his head. "This is a bad plan."

Luke shrugged. "I don't see another one."

Before long, Aces strolled into the diner. Luke caught his gaze and Aces walked to the table. "Hey, Spades. What's up?"

"Have a seat, Aces. Gibs and I have business to discuss with you."

Aces slid his tall body into the chair and the waitress brought him coffee. When she left, Aces looked over the table to Luke. "Why'd you call me here, Spades?"

"You got Gibs into a bit of trouble." There was no friggin' way he was going to beat around the bush.

"What're you talking about?"

"Don't bullshit me, Aces. If you needed transportation you should have talked to me."

"Again," growled Aces, "what the fuck are you talking about?"

"I don't talk about it, but ten years ago I hung around with the Rojos. I still have connections there."

"Yeah, right," spit Aces. He glanced around, suddenly interested in who else might be at the diner.

"No, Aces." Gibs finally found his voice. "It's true. They called Luke to their clubhouse today to ask him what the hell's going on. They consider him the eyes on Hades' Spawn."

Luke shrugged. He was Hades' Spawn but... "It's how we live and let live. The Rojos know damn well that Hades' Spawn has a rep in Tucson. Hell, the Rojos club in Tucson had dust-ups with the Spawn. You know all about that, don't you, Aces?"

Aces' eyes grew wide. "What the fuck you talking about, Spade?"

Luke leaned over. "Look, you asshole, the Spawn may have pushed around the Rojos in Tucson, but they're associated with the fucking Hombres here. Blood brothers. You mess with the Rojos you mess with a fucking organization of the most brutal killers in gang history. Hell. They kill for their own president on a yearly basis. You think Lil' Ricki is in Enfield because he got caught at something? He wanted to get caught just to put a wall of concrete and barbed wire between him and his own gang. You think being part of a one percenters club is going to protect you? These people have thousands, and I mean thousands, of members who literally kill to get into their organization. None of this skull and crossbones crap where you get a patch when you kill for the club. They don't need no patch to announce they killed someone. If they are wearing a Rojos patch or Hombres colors you can be sure they got it by killing someone."

Aces leaned back in his chair and hooked an arm around the back. He gave a hard stare to Luke as if he was reassessing him. "What's your point, Spades?"

"The Rojos are pissed you pulled this crap, trying to cut them out of their business."

"I was just exploiting a business opportunity."

Good. He admitted to it. "You were fucking set up to take the fall for some bullshit move from an Hombre looking to cover his own ass. Maybe the cops caught him or maybe he's just making some sideways play to move up in the organization. In any case, he's trying to take the heat off him and put it on someone else. But the person you're dealing with in the Hombres is an informant for the police. And you, asshole, fell for it hook, line and sinker."

"Fuck you, Wade," snarled Aces, leaning forward in his chair.

Luke leaned in also, nearly coming nose to nose with Aces. "Oh yeah, I'm fucked, and so is Gibs, and everyone else in the club if you don't produce the Hombre you've been 'doing business' with. More than fucked. The Rojos'll kill every last one of us. They won't ask questions."

Chapter Eighteen

Escape

Emily returned from speaking to Mrs. Diggerty about Reger. The dear woman was happy to take care of her cat for an extended period, and right now the tabby was exploring Mrs. Diggerty's apartment, making himself at home.

The elderly woman had been shocked to learn Evan had entered the building and the first thing she did was call a locksmith to have the front door and Emily's locks replaced. Emily apologized over and over to Mrs. Diggerty for causing so much trouble, but the dear woman shushed her.

"I've gotten too lax about these things. I should have put in a security system years ago. I'll make some calls and see who I can get in here to install one."

"But the cost, Mrs. Diggerty. You shouldn't have to..."

"Emily, dear. Don't worry. I've saved every dime of the rent on that apartment. I have plenty of money. Besides, a security system will lower my insurance payments."

"But you said you needed the first floor apartment to make the bills."

"And I do. But I save the money from the small apartment. It's my rainy day fund."

Emily didn't feel good about leaving Mrs. Diggerty with her cat and an empty apartment she couldn't pay for. However, she was glad the elderly woman had her life so well ordered that she wasn't going to suffer for Emily's problems. She only wished that eventually she could do the same with hers.

She had no idea how much to pack or what, but she decided to keep things light. A couple pairs of jeans, some t-shirts, a few thin polyester dresses and panties would get her through the next week or so. Emily pulled out a pair of strap sandals to wear with the dresses and packed a few toiletries and her makeup. All of this went into a duffle, which she could sling on her back if she rode a motorbike.

"Emily! Emily!"

She heard through her living room window. "What the—?" Emily froze. *No! It couldn't be. Please no!* She looked out the window to see Evan standing there shouting.

"Get out here, Emily. I need to talk to you! I know you're home!"

Quickly, Emily dialed 911. "Dispatch. What's the emergency?"

"My ex-boyfriend is outside in violation of a protective order. Please send someone! Hurry!"

"Who's calling?"

"Emily Dougherty."

"And your ex-boyfriend's name?"

"Evan Waters. Please, he was already in my apartment once today."

"You let him in?"

"No. He broke in." Emily's breathing kicked into high gear as she began to hyperventilate. She couldn't talk, though the woman kept asking questions.

"Are you okay? Tell me what's happening, Emily."

Frantically, Emily moved to the kitchen to find a paper bag. Lightheaded, she swayed and bumped into the cabinets. Finally, she found a bag and sinking to the kitchen floor buried her face in it. She was exhausted by the time her breathing calmed and she didn't think she could get up from the floor.

She heard a knock on the door and her heart sped up again. It couldn't be Evan. He couldn't be that stupid. She hadn't heard sirens so it couldn't be police. They never seemed to arrive on time these days. Or maybe it just felt like forever all the time now.

"Emily. It's Saks, Luke's friend. Are you there?"

"Oh goodness! Thank you, Lord!" Emily got up on shaky legs and stumbled to the door.

A tall, thin man stood in the doorway. His hair was dark and stylishly cut. Wearing jeans and a white V-neck tee, aside from his leather club jacket, he looked as clean cut as any man in her church. His brown eyes widened when he saw her. "Are you okay? You look as pale as a ghost."

"Did you see him?" She glanced anxiously over Saks' shoulder, standing on her tippie toes to peer over him.

"Who?"

"Evan, my ex. He was just outside shouting my name."

"No. I didn't." Saks frowned. "It's a good thing I got here now. You have a bag?"

"Yes."

"Where is it?"

"The bedroom." She pointed toward it.

Saks moved quickly and grabbed it up. "Anything else you need?"

"No. Yes." Emily grabbed up her purse and her phone.

"Got the charger for that thing?" asked Saks.

"Oh, shoot." Emily grabbed that from a drawer in one of the end tables.

"Let's go before the idiot decides to return."

"I called the police."

"Well, let's get going before they show up. They'll keep us here with stupid questions and Luke wants us to make tracks."

They hardly made it out of the front door when Evan appeared from the side of the house and stood in the walkway that led to the house.

"Emily!"

"Go away, Evan. I have a protective order and the police are on the way."

"Drop this bullshit, Emily. This protective order's stupid. We can work things out. I can forgive all your stupidity."

Saks gave Evan a stare that said 'drop dead'.

"Not after the crap you pulled, Evan." She was about to push past him when she stopped. "What the hell was your idea of coming into my apartment and spray painting bitch on my door? Was that supposed to endear me to you? How'd you get into my apartment in the first place?"

Evan sneered. "You can't prove anything."

"Do I need to? You've showed me your true colors already. I don't need proof to know what kind of man you are."

"You are a bitch. A stupid little bitch with the hots for jerks like that." He nodded towards Saks.

Saks crossed his arms over his chest and stared down his nose at Evan.

Emily didn't give him a chance to speak. "Who I like is none of your business. Not anymore. Get out of my way."

"Slut," snapped Evan.

"Move your ass," said Saks warningly.

"Who's this, Emily? Someone else you're fucking?"

"Get out of the way, Evan," she warned. "We're through. You're just making things worse for yourself. It's over." Emily stepped forward and Evan grabbed her arm.

"I said I needed to talk to you. I might drop the charges—"

Saks stepped between them. "Get your hand off her, asshole. She doesn't want to talk to you."

"Who the fuck are you?"

"The man who'll take your hands off of her if you don't do it."

"Damn, Emily. You sure can pick them." Evan glared at Saks and tightened his hold on Emily's arm.

"I won't tell you again." Saks' voice was low, full of warning.

"Go ahead, tough guy."

Everything suddenly happened in a blur. Saks stepped in quickly and shoved the heel of his hand into Evan's jaw. Evan staggered back, breaking his hold on Emily. She jumped away with a shriek as Saks advanced on Evan again. Evan swung wildly and Saks grabbed Evan's arm with his right hand, threw his left elbow into Evan's chin. He spun Evan around by pulling hard on Evan's outstretched hand. Saks threw his left arm around Evan's neck and jerked hard, pinning Evan in place against Saks' body.

"Okay, asshole. I'm giving you one last chance to walk away. You don't do it, I'll pound you in the ground. I haven't had my pounding today and that makes me plenty cranky. Are you going to walk away?"

"Yeah, sure," Evan gasped.

"What was that?"

"Yes, sir."

Saks pushed Evan away, but Evan turned and launched himself back toward Saks.

"Saks!" screeched Emily as her ex landed a punch in Saks' gut. He grunted, but pulled Evan's head up by his hair and returned the gut punch. Evan fell on Saks and they both tumbled to the grass, wrestling on the ground.

"Stop! Stop!" Emily yelled, but both men didn't listen.

Police sirens pierced the air and grew louder.

"Saks! Let's go!"

Her erstwhile rescuer scrambled to his feet and Evan grabbed at his ankles. Saks did a half hop out of Evan's hands, turned, and kicked Evan in the gut.

Evan groaned and Saks grabbed Emily's bag.

"Come on, girl," he said. He ran towards his bike parked in the street as Evan cursed at them. Saks climbed on the bike and fired it up. He handed the bag to Emily and she stuffed her phone and purse in it and slung it on her back, then settled in the bitch seat behind Saks and threw her arms around his waist.

Evan was on his feet now as the police sirens moved achingly close.

"Go ahead. Run away you coward. You'll be fucking sorry!" screamed Evan as Saks and Emily pulled away on the road.

Saks took it nice and easy on the street as the police cruisers streaked by them and pulled up at Emily's apartment house.

Emily looked back to see Evan talking to the police officers animatedly, pointing his hands in her direction. For once, the slowness of the local police worked in Emily's favor as Saks moved out of her neighborhood and onto the main road taking her away from the mess that was Evan Waters.

Saks brought Emily to a small, neatly kept suburban Westfield house. A white picket fence surrounded a cottage-sized house painted gray with white trim. Black shutters graced either side of the windows and the door was a burgundy red.

They rumbled into the driveway to a graceful stop. Emily sat back and took in her surroundings. "Is this your house?"

"No. It's Gibs'. I figured it would be better to come here in case that asshole took down my bike's plate. Come on."

Emily followed Saks to a side door and he knocked. A woman Emily recognized from Luke's apartment bobbed her head in the window and opened the door."

"Tony? What's going on? What happened to you? Is that blood on your forehead?"

"It's fine. Don't worry about me. This is Luke's girl, Emily. She needs a place to stay until Luke can pick her up."

"Hello, Helen."

"Emily! It's nice to see you again. Come on in. Would you like some ice tea?"

"I've got to go and take care of some business at the shop." Saks looked eager to disappear now.

"Nonsense. You come in this house right now Anthony Parks, and let me look at that forehead."

Saks sighed and entered the house behind Emily. Helen pointed to the kitchen table and they sat. Emily could see darkened places on Saks' face, and blood dripping from a cut on his head.

"It's nothing," he protested as Helen pressed a wet washcloth against the cut.

"Shush," said Helen. "What did you get into?"

"Saks was defending me against my ex-boyfriend," said Emily. "I've a protective order but the jerk won't leave me alone."

"Humph," said Helen as she applied a steri-strip to Saks' forehead. "You'll live, of course, you hard-headed fool. That's swelling nicely. Here is some ice to hold against it. Go lay down on the couch while I talk with Emily."

Saks glanced at the door. "But—"

"You know better than to argue with me. Go!"

Chapter Nineteen

The Plan

"You sure laid it on thick," said Gibs after Aces left.

The club president had left swearing and spitting warnings about drumming Luke and Gibs out of Hades' Spawn.

"Who said I was laying it on thick, Gibs?" Luke spoke these words, his jaw set as if he was preparing for battle. "Every word I said was true. The Rojos won't stand for someone cutting in on their territory. They're armed for violence and have no problem using it. In fact, they take pleasure in other people's pain." Luke took the last sip of his coffee, then stared at Gibs. "Is there someplace Helen can go for a while?"

Gibs' face lost some of its color. "Sh-She has her job, she needs..."

"To get somewhere safe," finished Luke.

"Oh fuck," muttered Gibs.

"In fact, if we were smart, we'd get out of Connecticut, but that would only get us so far. The Rojos have long memories. Besides which, I have to get you to your court date." Luke settled his coffee cup back in its saucer, a thoughtful expression on his face.

"What if we go to the police?" said Gibs. "Get some sort of protection deal."

"I'm not going back under witness protection," said Luke grimly.

"Back?" said Gibs.

"Why do you think you never heard about my parents, Gibs, eh? They're both dead. The program couldn't protect them. In the end, they shipped me across the country, stuck me in foster care, and told me adios." He stared at Gibs. "No one knows my real name. And no one is going to. Hell, not even my birthday is my real birthday, the shit was that deep."

"Holy mother." Gibs stared at him wide eyed. "How long has this been going on? You know shit, don't you? Stuff from before?" He held his hand up. "Don't tell me. I don't even want to know."

"All I've ever done is run. I'm so fucking tired of running." Luke sighed, long and hard. "So, we are going to get this shit cleared up with the Rojos, even if that means I have to feed Aces to them on a goddamn platter. In the meantime, we've got to get Helen out of the line of fire. But where can she go?"

"The only place Helen ever would go is on a cruise."

"Seriously?"

"Yeah, one of those Caribbean cruises."

"That's not a half bad idea."

"I can't afford something like that."

"Well, that's what credit cards are for. I guess that's something else you'll have to pay back to me."

"Luke," said Gibs. "I haven't told Helen what's going on. She's not going to understand me sending her on a cruise without me going."

A chirping noise erupted from Luke's pocket. He pulled out his phone and stared at it, then he shook his head. "She's a saint, you know? I'd have kicked your ass from here to Hartford by now. It's about fucking time you start telling her the truth, Gibs."

"Yeah," Gibs muttered.

"Saks just texted me. He took Emily to your house. More bullshit with her ex." Luke stood and put his hand on Gibs' shoulder. "Let's go, Lucy. You've got some 'splaining' to do."

They traveled to Gibs' house side by side on their bikes. Gibs looked grim and Luke didn't blame him. Explaining to your wife that you were arrested with narcotics possession with intent to sell was a conversation Luke never wanted to have. And then trying to hide it? He was just glad he wasn't Gibs today.

The ride gave Luke a chance to think. He'd be surprised if Aces gave up his contact in the Hombres and wouldn't be surprised if the club president was already packing for a trip back to Tucson. That wouldn't get him out of trouble, just delay the inevitable. Still, people did stupid things all the time. Luke vowed not to be one of those people.

He thought of Emily and his heart sank. There was no way he could drag her through this with him. He loved her more than any other woman in his life, except for his mother. Shit was getting deep and Luke had no idea if he was going to make it out of this alive.

Many times during his life he faced the possibility of dying. When his parents were murdered, he was at school. A Witsec agent dragged him out of the classroom, loaded him into the back of an SUV and drove him to the airport. Luke, being eight, threw a fit. The bastard pulled the vehicle over onto the side of the road, leaned over his seat and proceeded to read Luke the riot act. More like yell.

"Listen, kid. I ain't playing. Shut your mouth. You can't go home because there's no home to go to. Your parents are dead, both of them. Your old man just couldn't play by the rules and was in shit so deep they'll be looking for you next. So be quiet and let me get you out of here so you don't end up like them."

That was Luke's first brush with death. The news his parents were dead and what the man said terrified his eight-year-old self. In a sense, Luke died on that day.

Then landing in the foster home was a different kind a death, a place where people called him by a name he didn't recognize, speaking a language he barely knew. The next was the motorcycle accident he had with Emily. Luke didn't tell Emily the true extent of his injuries, but they had to remove his spleen to keep him from bleeding out internally. The last time was when he woke up in the Rojos' clubhouse with the dead club member next to him. Maybe it took him a while to get the message, but he finally got it that day.

The Navy provided a kind of a home, but he still felt disconnected from his fellow sailors. The officers seemed to have it out for Luke and he didn't like kissing their asses. Witsec, not paying attention to him for about a decade, lost track of him when he joined the Navy. Or maybe they thought that being in the Navy was a way for them not to have to pay attention to him. When Luke got out he started his relatively quiet life and no one bothered him except the occasional Rojos looking to make points, and that wasn't till after he met Okie. Meeting Okie and joining the Spawn was a turning point in his life. He felt for the second time in his life he found a home. The first time was when he fell in love with Emily. Now his club and the love of his life were in jeopardy, and it was hard to see if things were going to work out so he could have both the club and her. Or either of them.

Keeping Emily in his life after all this would be plain selfish, not to mention dangerous for her. He had to face it. To keep her safe he'd have to do the one thing he didn't ever want to do.

They pulled into Gibs' driveway and parked the bikes. Both lost in thoughts of their own, they slowly walked into Gibs' house.

Helen sat at the kitchen table with Emily smiling and joking with her and Saks. When the two men entered through the side door, however, the atmosphere turned somber when the three at the table saw the look on Luke and Gibs' faces.

"Make it fast, Gibs." Luke pushed his friend gently forward.

"Right. Helen, I've got to talk to you." Gibs began cracking his knuckles.

"What's going on, Frank?"

Luke looked at Saks and nodded his head towards the living room. "Keep an eye out that window while I talk with Emily?"

Saks didn't say a word, just got up and moved to the living room.

"It's that bad?" Emily looked exhausted but still beautiful.

He'd never get tired of looking at her. He tried to burn her image into his head, hoping the picture would never fade. He held his hand out to her. She took it and followed him into a small bedroom that didn't look regularly used. Luke closed the door.

"What's going on, Luke?"

"I can't tell you all of it without making you an accessory, so I won't. You've got enough trouble on your hands, and I won't make it worse for you. I'm sorry. I'm so sorry for everything that is going down, and sorry for the problems you're having, and just plain sorry that this isn't working out."

"Wait... what?!" She took a step closer to him. "You said... you said we could work this out together."

Luke shook his head. "There are things you just don't know about me, Em, and as much as I hate to say it, those things make it impossible for us to be together."

"Then don't say it. Don't say it, Luke! I'm sorry. I'm sorry I listened to my parents and let them drive me away from you. I can't lose you twice."

He hated breaking her heart. But broken was still beating. Any other choice he had would get her killed. "It's not about that, Em. It's never about that. I love you. I've always loved you and I always will. But I can't let you suffer by being with me."

"I don't!"

"You will."

Emily launched herself at Luke, crushing her lips against his. It was as if she thought that if she reminded him so painfully about what he wanted, that he'd change his mind.

Luke wrapped his arms around her as her sweet scent filled his nostrils. She didn't need perfume to smell sexy to him. Just the press of her body against him made him hard and he wanted nothing more than to be buried deep inside her. Her breathing hitched as she sought his tongue with hers and pressed her hips against his. Good heavens, feeling her lean into his cock drove him crazy.

"I want you," she whispered in his ear. "I need you."

And he needed her. Just the thought that he'd never get to do this again drove him beyond reason. When her hands undid his belt, he didn't stop her. As she pushed down his jeans, he quickly pushed down his boxers, setting his cock free. He leaned into her again, pushing her against the closed door. She didn't even wait for him to do it. Emily pushed down her little lacy panties, letting them fall to the floor. He brought his hand between her thighs and felt her succulent juices between them. In his minds-eye he pictured her folds glistening and inviting him to enter her.

He lifted her against the door and she hooked her legs around his hips. With one hand he guided his cock to her soft, wet lips, rubbing the tip against them until he found her entrance. He didn't wait. Luke entered, pulling her down on top of him. She whimpered and he wasn't sure if she liked it or that he took her too fast.

"Fuck me, baby," she whispered hoarsely.

The door rattled and he moved them both to the wall. But when he did, he pushed into her hard, and then pulled back, and then again, driving towards a rhythm that drove him higher. All thoughts were on her, the softness between her legs clenching him, pushing him to pour all of himself into her. There was nothing else but this place and this time, her taking all of him and he needing to give it.

Her breathing hitched and he knew she was close. He pulled her head to his shoulder and he felt her scream into it as she broke apart. The clenching of her muscles pulsing around his shaft drove him insane. He couldn't hold back and he didn't want to. Sparks flashed within his closed eyes. Joy and pleasure jolted through him as he exploded into her.

Luke held her tightly. She was the only treasure that meant anything to him.

"There, baby," she said breathily. "That's what matters. I love you."

Chapter Twenty

Double-cross

"Luke," Emily heard through the door. "It looks like things are getting a little too crowded out here."

"Right there, Saks." Luke slid his boxer briefs back on and pulled his jeans quickly up his legs, careful of the bandage. His leg hadn't been bothering him but now he could feel it. It had been a long day and he didn't see any end to it yet. He belted his jeans and gave Emily a quick kiss.

"Sweetheart, things are going to move quickly. Get ready to fly."

Emily redressed and ran her fingers through her hair. "I'm ready, Luke."

He nodded and walked into the living room. He limped slightly but at least he didn't need his crutches. He hadn't used them at all today. There were more important things than a cut. It would heal. A scar would remain, but the wound would heal.

Saks leaned over the back of the couch and stared out to the street through the large curtained picture window.

Luke joined him. "What do we have?"

"See for yourself."

"Shit!" exclaimed Luke when he peered out cautiously onto the road.

"What is it?" Emily said, alarmed by Luke's reaction.

"Gibs!" called Luke.

"Yeah, Luke," said Gibs.

"You filled in Helen?"

"Yeah, she's putting some clothes together now."

"How'd it go?"

"You know how they say you have a fifty percent chance of getting divorced?"

"Yeah."

"For me the percentage went up a bit."

"I don't blame her," said Luke.

"Luke," said Emily more stridently, "what's going on?"

"We have visitors."

"Where," said Emily, walking close to the window.

Luke pulled her down on the couch.

"There."

Emily glanced out the window but didn't see anything but parked cars lining the opposite side of the street.

"There're just cars."

"Look again, see that old blue Cadillac?"

"Yeah?"

"The men inside don't belong on this street."

"Who do you think it is?" said Saks.

"Got to be Hombres. Rojos would be on their bikes." Luke pulled out his wallet. "Saks, here's my credit card. Take Helen up to Bradley, put her in the hotel there until we can get her on a flight out."

"Sure, boss."

"You stay with her, understand?"

"Yes."

"Go. Now."

Saks nodded and stood.

"Good luck, boss. Helen?" he called. "It's time to take a ride."

Saks disappeared into the kitchen and Emily turned to Luke.

"What's going on? Please tell me." She was terrified, trembling and shaking, her eyes wide.

"It's fucked up shit, Em. Our club president has been trying to do business with a local gang. Only in doing that he's been trying to cut out the people who actually do business with that gang. To make things worse, the guy working with Aces, our president, well, it's unsanctioned by his higher-ups. So we've got a bunch of pissed off gang bangers who think the Spawn are the cause of their troubles."

"I didn't realize—"

"Yeah," said Luke, peering out the window again. "Neither did I until today. That's what I get for not paying attention. So, I need to get us out of here before the shit gets deeper."

In the background a Harley rumbled to life. Emily swallowed hard, her problems with Evan seeming very small compared to what Luke faced. "How are you involved? Can you just tell them it wasn't you?" She shrugged, confused. "What makes this your fight?"

"Aces dragged Gibs into it. I think the fucker didn't quite trust his new associate and sent Gibs in to do what Aces should have. My employee. My club. My fight."

The Harley's engine roared and faded as it sped away.

Gibs walked into the room, all color drained from his face. "Okay," he said as calmly as if he took out the trash, "that's done."

"Good," said Luke.

"What about her?" Gibs said, nodding at Emily.

"I'm staying." Emily set her feet apart, as if preparing to fight.

"No. You're not." Luke avoided looking at her. "Gibs, pull your car out of the garage."

"Okay, Luke."

Emily gripped Luke's arms. "Don't send me away."

"You've got to go, babe. These fuckers don't play. You don't want to be here when this shit goes down. You can't."

It hit her then that Luke's life was in danger. Ice ran through her blood when she realized by the grim look on his face that he might not survive the night. She panicked then, thinking she might never see him again if she left him. The world slipped out of her control and the room spun. She fought the feeling. She could not lose it now.

"Baby?" said Luke.

Emily gasped, trying to steady herself. "This sucks. For ten years I've thought about nothing but you. I cried, Luke, more tears than I can count. And now when I have you again you want me to walk away?"

"That's right, baby. Because life would mean shit if something happened to you."

"Don't you get it? I feel the same way about you."

Luke leaned his forehead against hers. "I know."

Gibs burst into the room. "I was trying to get my bike moved when they pulled up. Fuck, Luke. The cops are here!"

"What!" Luke pulled aside the window's heavy curtains and saw two cruisers pulling up to the curb outside the house.

"Emily. You have to go. Now."

Emily looked at Luke, and her head spun as her breathing hitched. She didn't know if she could stand, let alone walk. She tried to say something when the sound of heavy pounding on the front door filled the room.

Luke nodded to Gibs. "Answer it."

Gibs walked to the front door and pulled it open to find two officers with guns drawn.

"Put your hands behind your head and get down on the floor," one of the officers spit out.

The older man did as he was told. "Mind telling me what this is about?"

"Shut up."

"No. This is my home. Tell me what this is about."

"Kidnapping," spit the other cop. "Where is she?"

"Kidnapping?" squeaked Emily. She found her feet and stood, turning to face the cops. "Who?"

"Are you Emily Dougherty?"

"Yes."

"Then you."

"What! Did you happen to get that from Evan Waters?"

The two cops looked at each other confirming Emily's suspicions. "Oh, for heaven's sakes!" she exploded. "And how did you find me? Eh?"

The cops stood mute and Emily realized that something was rotten.

"Did he pull some GPS shit on my phone? Did he?"

"So you're not here against your will?"

Luke pulled Emily against him. "Go with them, Em," he whispered in her ear. "Let them get you out of here. Please. For all our sakes."

"No," she said firmly.

Luke pushed her away. "Please officers, Take this crazy bitch off my hands. She keeps following me everywhere."

"Luke?!" protested Emily.

"That's right, officer," said Gibs, playing Luke's hand. "She's trespassing on my property. Forced her way in here. She ain't right. She out on bond for some shit."

"Gibs!"

"Yeah," said Luke. "You should take her to her parents' house. They'll keep an eye on her. It's eighteen oh two Faraway Court in Walkerville."

"We'll take her down to the station and call her parents. That is, if you're pressing charges."

"I am," said Gibs.

"No!" screamed Emily. This could not be happening!

"Come along, Miss. Don't make this harder than it has to be."

"Luke!" appealed Emily. He couldn't do this to her. He couldn't have the police haul her away.

The guttural roar of motorcycles split the air and Luke dove for the curtains once again.

"Fuck," he swore softly. "Rojos."

"Officers," said Gibs. "Can I get up from the floor now?"

An officer nodded and Gibs stood.

"Please, officers," said Luke, refusing to look at Emily, knowing her expression would break him. "Get that crazy bitch out of here."

"I'll need information to make a report," said one officer.

"We'll follow you down and make it at the police station," said Luke. "We've got company and we need to tell them to come back another time."

The officer looked at Luke doubtfully but put Emily's hands behind her back and zip tied them.

"Don't do this, please," begged Emily.

The officer pulled her to the door. "Let's go. Into the patrol car."

At that moment three motor bikes stopped in front of Gibs' house. Each rider wore denim cuts and red bandanas on their heads.

"These your friends?" said one cop doubtfully.

Luke stood and pushed by Emily and her cop escort onto the front lawn. Gibs followed him.

"What're you doing here, man?" Luke hissed. "Did you send those assholes to watch me?" He pointed to the blue Cadillac.

"What of it, 'omes?" said one of them.

"Not a good time." Luke jerked his head towards the two cops.

"Yeah. It ain't a good sign you talking to the cops."

"Has nothing to do with you or me, Sal," said Luke.

"Hard to tell, ese. You know that. In fact, I'm tired of your games." With that the man on the bike raised his hand, which was curled around a pistol.

"Gun!" shouted one of the cops. The cop who had his hand on Emily's arm shoved her back into the house, and they both pointed their weapons at the biker.

Emily dashed back to the picture window, her heart pounding. She pushed aside the curtains with her head to watch the frozen tableau before her. Luke had his hands raised and

Emily could hear him speaking to the biker who threatened him because the front door was still open.

"Not your best move, dude," warned Luke. "Drive off. Even if you shoot me, these cops will pop one in you."

The biker mumbled something, and then Gibs shouted, "Luke! Watch out!"

With horror Emily watched as three men poked their heads up in the Cadillac and pointed guns at the bikers. Gibs jumped in front of Luke as the men in the Cadillac fired at the bikers. Gibs fell, grunting. The man speaking to Luke fell off his bike. Luke fell to the ground.

"Luke!" Emily screamed, but it did no good. Luke lay on top of Gibs, holding the man's head. The other two bikers shot into the Cadillac.

Pop. Pop. Pop.

The air was filled with the furtive sound of gunfire. In the rain of bullets, the cops fired, hitting one of the other bikers. One, in the driver's seat in the Cadillac, leaned out of the window, his face a red mass of blood.

One of the cops spoke frantically into his shoulder radio calling for back-up.

"Shots fired. Shots fired," he spat into the mike urgently.

Emily had one thought. Luke. He lay on Gibs. His faced was contorted with pain.

Gibs lay under him, unmoving.

The last biker tore down the street and suddenly everything was quiet.

Too quiet.

Emily gasped at the savage scene. Two of the bikers were dead, their bikes toppled on top of them. The three men in the Cadillac were motionless.

Luke slowly got to his knees, his face contorted in grief. Gibs remained unmoving and that's when Emily realized Gibs was dead.

"Fuckers!" yelled Luke down the street. "You damn motherfuckers!"

"Get on the ground," screamed one of the cops.

"Fuck you! Fuck you!"

"Down on the ground!"

The commands of the cop were drowned in screaming sirens coming toward the scene of destruction. Emily got off the couch and ran past the cops toward Luke, but one of the cops caught her and held her back. "Luke!" she called.

He sunk to his knees laying his forehead on Gibs' chest.

The cop that held Emily pushed her down the walkway toward his car while the other one moved cautiously toward Luke, as if he was the criminal.

"Luke!" Emily cried as tears streamed down her face.

The cop put her in his patrol car locking her in the back seat. The other policeman attempted to get Luke to move away from Gibs, but Luke shook him off.

Police cars and ambulances stopped in the street with their lights flashing. Paramedics moved through the scene checking the downed men, and police stood talking in groups with each other. Emily wondered why they weren't doing anything. Just as she thought that, one uniformed man went to speak to the two cops on the scene.

Finally, at the urging of some of the newer cops and the paramedics that arrived, Luke stood. One of the newer cops took him aside to ask questions, but it was apparent Luke wasn't talking. Plain-clothes cops pulled up behind the black and whites and milled around asking questions. Finally, one went to Luke asking questions with his hands animated. He stepped in aggressively toward him.

Emily watched all this in a state of shock. She'd never seen a real-life scene of death and destruction, and it seemed to her the cops around her were equally confused.

Finally, one of the plain-clothes cops pulled open the patrol car door and Emily heard the voices around her. "What happened here, Miss?"

But Emily was drawn to Luke and what he was yelling.

"Fuck you, Anglotti. Where were you five fucking minutes ago?"

"Mr. Wade, if you don't cooperate, I'll arrest you for obstruction."

"Go right ahead, asshole. On the advice of my lawyer I'm staying silent. And I want to speak to him too."

"Come on then," said Anglotti. He pushed Luke to face away from him then pulled Luke's hands together to handcuff him.

Suddenly a black SUV drove up on the lawn from the side, knocking down a portion of the white picket fence. Two men jumped out, ran over to Luke and flashed some badges at Anglotti.

"Let go of him. We're taking him now."

"You can't do that. He's a material witness at the very least."

"Not anymore. Come on, Raymond. In the van. We've got to get you out of here before news cameras show up. We can't risk it."

Luke's eyes, filled with pain and anger, met Emily's, then turned away as the two men escorted Luke into the SUV.

She watched in complete shock as it pulled away. Her mind filled with more questions than answers.

Who were those men? What the hell was going on?

Why had they called him Raymond? Where were they taking him?

Would she ever see the man she loved again? Or had fate and circumstances taken him away from her this time forever?

THE END
One That Came Back - Coming October 2015

More by Lexy Timms:

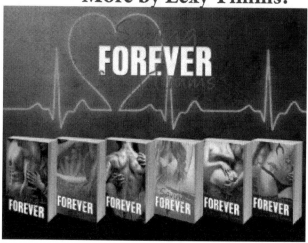

Book One is FREE!

**Sometimes the heart needs a different kind of saving...
find out if Charity Thompson will find a way of saving forever
in this hospital setting Best-Selling Romance by Lexy Timms**
Charity Thompson wants to save the world, one hospital at a
time. Instead of finishing med school to become a doctor, she
chooses a different path and raises money for hospitals – new
wings, equipment, whatever they need. Except there is one
hospital she would be happy to never set foot in again—her
fathers. So of course he hires her to create a gala for his sixty-fifth
birthday. Charity can't say no. Now she is working in the one
place she doesn't want to be. Except she's attracted to Dr. Elijah
Bennet, the handsome playboy chief.
Will she ever prove to her father that's she's more than a med
school dropout? Or will her attraction to Elijah keep her from
repairing the one thing she desperately wants to fix?
** This is NOT Erotica. It's Romance and a love story. **

* This is Part 1 of a Five book Romance Series. It does end on a cliffhanger*

Heart of the Battle Series
Celtic Viking
Book 1
Celtic Rune
Book 2
Celtic Mann
Book 3

In a world plagued with darkness, she would be his salvation.
No one gave Erik a choice as to whether he would fight or not. Duty to the crown belonged to him, his father's legacy remaining beyond the grave.
Taken by the beauty of the countryside surrounding her, Linzi would do anything to protect her father's land. Britain is under attack and Scotland is next. At a time she should be focused on suitors, the men of her country have gone to war and she's left to stand alone.
Love will become available, but will passion at the touch of the enemy unravel her strong hold first?
Fall in love with this Historical Celtic Viking Romance.
* There are 3 books in this series. Book 1 will end on a cliff hanger.
*Note: this is NOT erotica. It is a romance and a love story.

Knox Township, August 1863.

Little Love Affair, Book 1 in the Southern Romance series, by bestselling author Lexy Timms

Sentiments are running high following the battle of Gettysburg, and although the draft has not yet come to Knox, "Bloody Knox" will claim lives the next year as citizens attempt to avoid the Union draft. Clara's brother Solomon is missing, and Clara has been left to manage the family's farm, caring for her mother and her younger sister, Cecelia.

Meanwhile, wounded at the battle of Monterey Pass but still able to escape Union forces, Jasper and his friend Horace are lost and starving. Jasper wants to find his way back to the Confederacy, but feels honor-bound to bring Horace back to his family, though the man seems reluctant.

NOTE: This is romance series, book 1 of 4

The Recruiting Trip

Aspiring college athlete Aileen Nessa is finding the recruiting process beyond daunting. Being ranked #10 in the world for the 100m hurdles at the age of eighteen is not a fluke, even though she believes that one race, where everything clinked magically together, might be. American universities don't seem to think so. Letters are pouring in from all over the country.

As she faces the challenge of differentiating between a college's genuine commitment to her or just empty promises from talent-seeking coaches, Aileen heads to the University of Gatica, a Division One school, on a recruiting trip. Her best friend dares who to go just to see the cute guys on the school's brochure.

The university's athletic program boasts one of the top hurdlers in the country. Tyler Jensen is the school's NCAA champion in the hurdles and Jim Thorpe recipient for top defensive back in football. His incredible blue-green eyes, confident smile and rock hard six pack abs mess with Aileen's concentration.

His offer to take her under his wing, should she choose to come to Gatica, is a temping proposition that has her wondering if she might be with an angel or making a deal with the devil himself.

COMING SOON:

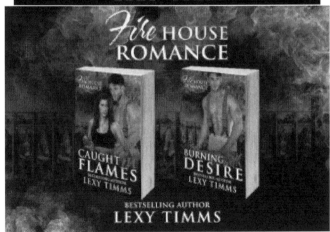

Hades' Spawn Motorcycle Club Series

One You Can't Forget
Book 1
One That Got Away
Book 2
One That Came Back
Book 3
Coming Fall 2015

Find Lexy Timms:

Lexy Timms Newsletter:
http://eepurl.com/9i0vD
Lexy Timms Facebook Page:
https://www.facebook.com/SavingForever
Lexy Timms Website:
http://lexytimms.wix.com/savingforever

Did you love *One That Got Away*? Then you should read *The Boss* by Lexy Timms!

From Best Selling Author, Lexy Timms, comes a billionaire romance that'll make you swoon and fall in love all over again.

Jamie Connors has given up on finding a man. Despite being smart, pretty, and just slightly overweight, she's a magnet for the kind of guys that don't stay around.

Her sister's wedding is at the foreground of the family's attention. Jamie would be find with it if her sister wasn't pressuring her to lose weight so she'll fit in the maid of honor dress, her mother would get off her case and her ex-boyfriend wasn't about to become   her   brother-in-law.

Determined to step out on her own, she accepts a PA position from billionaire Alex Reid. The job includes an apartment on his property and gets her out of living in her parent's basement.

Jamie has to balance her life and somehow figure out how to manage her billionaire boss, without falling in love with him.

** The Boss is book 1 in the Managing the Bosses series. All your questions won't be answered in the first book. It may end on a cliff   hanger.

For mature audiences only. There are adult situations, but this is a love story, NOT erotica.

Also by Lexy Timms

Hades' Spawn Motorcycle Club
One You Can't Forget
One That Got Away

Heart of the Battle Series
Celtic Viking
Celtic Rune
Celtic Mann

Managing the Bosses Series
The Boss

Saving Forever
Saving Forever - Part 1
Saving Forever - Part 2
Saving Forever - Part 3
Saving Forever - Part 4
Saving Forever - Part 5
Saving Forever - Part 6

Southern Romance Series
Little Love Affair
Siege of the Heart
Freedom Forever
Soldier's Fortune

Tennessee Romance
Whisky Lullaby

The University of Gatica Series

The Recruiting Trip
Faster
Higher
Stronger

Standalone
Wash
Loving Charity
Summer Lovin'
Love & College
Billionaire Heart
First Love

Made in the USA
Middletown, DE
20 July 2024

57752758R00099